The Adventures of Clark Westfield

The Cassandra Unit

By Tom Albright

ISBNs:

Paperback: 979-8-9888227-0-7
Hardcover: 979-8-9888227-1-4
EBook:979-8-9888227-2-1
Audio Book: 979-8-9888227-3-8

Table of Contents

Chapter 1

July 4th, 1976 – Eight-year-old Clark Westfield bent down to tie his shoe. The long-frayed shoelace on his Zips sneakers had already gotten caught in the chain of his blue Schwinn Stingray bicycle once. After young Clark had managed to untangle it without falling onto the pavement, he needed to make sure it wouldn't happen twice. He steadied himself in the center of the Cul De Sac at the top of the hill of Ellen court. It was a short suburban street where a developer had managed to put a dozen houses in the 1960's, eliminating yet another patch of woods and cultivating yet another neighborhood of white middle class families whose breadwinners commuted to New York City each morning. Two neighborhood children zoomed around the cul de sac on their bicycles – one was a portly seven-year-old named Chris

Ratti. Chris rode an Evel Knievel bike which was adorned with American flags and stickers showing the famous daredevil soaring over the Grand Canyon on his motorcycle.

At that moment, as eight-year-old Clark gauged the hill and prepared for his inaugural ride through the neighborhood on the hot July day, the world seemed to stand still for just a moment. It was Clark and his bicycle and summer perfection. The mind of an eight-year-old boy is an uncomplicated place where a simple quiet street with a hill represents a special type of freedom without limits. Once he was finished tying and double knotting his shoelace the only thing that mattered to Clark was beating Chris Ratti down the hill to prove the superiority of his new sparkling blue banner of childhood prestige. Like a heavyweight boxing champion about to start a drag race, he yelled to the adjacent child on the red, white and blue toy bike:

"OK Ratti – you are going to eat my dust going down this hill!" Clark smiled as he shouted his declaration though his conviction was serious. Chris Ratti made a salute and positioned his bicycle for the race. As the rest of the world celebrated the 200th anniversary of the Declaration of Independence, four small feet took to pedals and young hamstrings strained to turn the sprocket gears and outride one another. Clark felt the hot breeze on his face and in his hair as he took the lead down the short hill. His quadriceps strained and pumped to pedal harder and faster until it was clear he had long left his opponent behind. A glance under his armpit saw Chris Ratti behind him in the distance only halfway down the Ellen court hill, huffing and puffing his oversized child's frame on his ridiculous piece of novelty merchandise. Clark had won. He smiled. He leisurely steered the long handlebars into the driveway of house number 11 as the kinetic momentum from the hill let him ascend upwards towards the open garage doors. The bicycle with the boy on it glided into the dark garage forcing Clark's eyes to adjust to the sudden absence of sunlight. As the shapes around him became more obvious he suddenly tried to activate the coaster brakes but it was far too late to stop the careening bicycle. The front wheel slammed into a plastic milk crate filled with several pairs of shoes and launched the back of the bicycle and all 90 pounds of eight-year-old Clark Westfield forward until he slid off the silver banana seat into the rack of plywood shelves against the far end of the garage. His face hit the two by four that supported a particle board shelf someone had banged together, and his forehead landed against the soft cardboard of a large file box. In an effort to steady himself and not fall to the ground, he grabbed the top of the cardboard box, and it began to slide forward. Realizing the box had no leverage and he was in a virtual free fall, Clark fell sideways to the ground as the heavy box landed on top of him and toppled on its side, its contents of papers and manila folders spilling everywhere along the garage floor. Clark sat on the floor getting his bearings and rubbing his face where it had impacted with the wood. He lifted the bicycle and freed himself from under it, finding his shoelace mangled into the chain and sprocket once again. Papers were everywhere, they had been thrown around the garage floor as if a hurricane had hit. Clark sighed. He had beaten Chris Ratti down the hill on his new bike, only to crash in his own garage. A quick glance outside revealed Ratti at the foot of the driveway, aimlessly pedaling in circles. Clark began to pick up the papers and folders that had scattered themselves all over the floor. They were everywhere, some had floated over and landed square on the oil stain that marked the middle of the concrete floor. The oil seeped upward and began to stain the pages. Clark looked at the mess over the floor and sighed as the size of the pickup job sunk in. Not only would he have to pick up each of the explosion of pages from all over the garage he would have to make an attempt to put them back in order. He began gathering all the typed pages and putting them together in a stack that he figured he would sort out later.

Clark touched his face where it had impacted with the shelf. He winced. It hurt and as he looked at his hand it revealed a tiny spot of blood. He would need to go inside and get ice like his mother gave him every time he had a bruise. But he needed to clean up this crazy mess first. He found what seemed to be the first page of a thick stack that had fanned out on the floor somewhat in order. At the top was the logo for the State of New Jersey with those words written in classic calligraphy, under it were two scales, the scales of justice and the words Superior Court of New Jersey in a straight line. On the left side of the page in vertical type stacking were the words "State of New Jersey Vs. Joseph MacDougal" before double spaced typed lines of words made up the rest of the page. Clark stacked the pages as best he could. They weren't numbered. Among the random sheets was a different two paged stapled letter that had been folded in three to fit in an envelope. "This letter is a notification to the administrative office of the courts that Clark Westfield, Esquire, will be representing Joseph MacDougal as legal counsel…" While young Clark didn't understand what most of the letter meant, he recognized his father's name which was the same as his. Clark's father was an attorney and worked in an office two towns away. From what he could understand the letter seemed to say that Clark's father would be appearing as the lawyer for whoever Joseph MacDougal was.

Then Clark saw it….

In the middle of the strewn papers was an 8x10 photograph that had landed face up. It lay in the middle of the floor and as Clark stood over it a feeling of tension began to quicken in his abdomen. It was a closeup of the face of a young boy – roughly Clark's age – bruised, bloody and his eyes were shut. One eye was so severely bruised it was swollen like a purple golf ball almost black at the center. His eye was completely closed and dried blood formed a sticky trickling line down into his hair which was clumped together with dried blood. Clark didn't know what or who the picture was, but he immediately felt that somehow this must have been a real boy. Several additional full-page photos lay strewn next to the shot of his bloodied face. Trembling, Clark turned over one after another. They all showed the same horrible images – a severely bruised and bloody young male child. He was grade school age – probably second grade – and his pants were off. The shirt that remained was covered in blood and mud, it was completely discolored from the trauma and whatever circumstances surrounded these awful images. Clark felt a deep sick feeling as he gathered up the pictures and stacked them in his hands. He could feel his heart pounding in his chest and a non-descript nausea in the pit of his stomach. Why were these awful photos in a box in the garage of his home?

Some papers were strewn about as well. Some were yellowed around the edges the way typing paper discolors when exposed to humidity. Clark began to read some of the printed text on one of the pages: "The Defendant stated that after committing the murder and realizing the victim was definitely deceased, he sat quietly for several minutes before deciding he would have to hide the victim and decided to drive and find a secluded area…" Clark continued leafing through the typed pages until he found what looked like a first page. The upper half of the page was blank. Midway down on the left side was typed "The State of New Jersey vs. Joseph MacDougal" in marquis style spacing, followed by a dense legal jargon filled paragraph that Clark could not understand. He saw that the pages were numbered in the lower right corner, so he started to put them in order. As he handled page three, he saw words that gave him a further chill down his spine "The Defendant is represented by Clark Westfield Sr. Esq.". This was Clark's father who was an attorney, so that must have meant this was his case. Clark felt a second surge of deep sickness overtake him. It wasn't fear in the classic fight or flight sense, but a chemical surge of adrenaline and all other bodily chemicals that make you hyper alert and anxious, as everything around suddenly seems brighter, louder and more urgent. Clark was only 8 years old, but he knew that his father, in his work as a lawyer, sometimes had to deal with criminals. He had many talks with his father about why even if someone is guilty of a crime they still need and deserve to have a lawyer in court. But Clark had long thought that the worst of these "criminals" his father had to work with were bank robbers or car thieves. It never occurred to young Clark Westfield that any human being could be capable of doing such a horrible thing to someone else – let alone a nice young boy his age. He finished stacking the papers in order and neatly stacking the photos, placing both in the cardboard box that he had knocked off the shelf. He would just put it back in the spot from where it had fallen and try to forget he had ever seen it.

The garage door that led inside the house into the kitchen opened and Clark's mother called over to him: "Clark come in and have something to eat.." she shut the door without paying much attention. He picked up his bicycle and depressed the kickstand, balancing it in the standing position. He walked into his house through the kitchen where several pots boiled on the stove with various contents emitting various smells. His mother was nowhere to be found. The television blared a baseball game in the adjacent family room, with the sports announcer's even toned monotonous voice discussing obscure statistics and other details in which no person ever seemed interested. Clark walked cautiously into the room as if he had been caught doing something wrong. His father sat on the end of the couch closest to the television set, an empty plate with crumbs rested on a tray stand in front of Clark senior. Without thinking and without hesitation, young Clark blurted out to his father:

"Dad – what are those photos in the garage of the dead boy and why are they there?" he asked, drawing a quick glance from his father who after several seconds turned to give his son his full attention.

"What photos? What were you looking at?" asked the senior Westfield.

"The ones of the bloody dead boy in the cub scout uniform. It looked like one of your work files or something," replied Clark in a weak voice.

"Why were you looking through those?" asked Clark's father in a stern but non angry tone.

"Well, I raced Chris Ratti down the hill and when I rode my bike into the garage it was really dark, and I hit the shelves and that box fell over and everything spilled out and there are all these photos of…"

"Yeah, I know the photos. That's the crime scene and autopsy photos of the Della Russo boy. They were from a case I had to work on back in 1973," explained Clark's father. "You don't need to go looking through those Clark, those are from a terrible crime." His father now had a look of concern.

"Is that the boy who is on that monument down at the church?" asked Clark. He was referring to a stone memorial outside the local Catholic church that had a polished portrait of the Della Russo boy in his school uniform. Clark had seen the stone monument hundreds of times and read the inscription that read "Now with the angels after being abducted". As a little boy in the grade school or at church services, he had asked his mother and his grandmother about the picture and the boy several times. His mother had once replied that the boy was "somebody everyone loved who was no longer with us," which confused him. Clark's father paused for a moment and turned the volume off on the television. The baseball game fell silent.

"Yes, that's the boy from the monument at the church," replied Clark's father slowly. "He lived here in town and was murdered before we moved here. I was one of the lawyers that worked for the defendant."

"The defendant is the guy who did it right?" asked Clark. He was shocked his father would have any connection to such a horrible thing. It was upsetting at some level.

"Well in this case yes, the defendant is the bad guy and he admitted it," explained Mr. Westfield. "But not always."

"Why did you become his lawyer if he killed that boy, dad?" asked Clark completely baffled. Mr. Westfield addressed the child's question with the respect and sensitivity it deserved.

"Every person is entitled to representation. Even guilty people need a lawyer. A lawyer doesn't excuse what the person did, they only make sure they are handled properly by the legal system," he explained to young Clark. "I simply made sure he was treated fairly, and his rights were respected, and they were. We have to treat everyone fairly – even when they do terrible things. It's how we know we will be treated fairly if we ever wind up in court for any reason" 8-year-old Clark sat wide eyed in several moments of silence letting his father's words soak in.

"But he did all that stuff to him right? He killed him? And why didn't he have any pants on?" asked Clark after understanding that lawyers were necessary even for bad guys. The elder Westfield paused, searching for the right words with the fatherly wisdom that he needed to be honest about the gravity of what Clark had found but also explain it in a way that didn't traumatize the 8-year-old. Life's ugliest epiphanies almost always arrive as an ambush.

"Well Clark, I'll tell you the whole story because I know you are man enough to understand things," said his father, leading with affirmation. "First, you have to understand that people are generally good – even though some people do very bad things. Also, even though this happened right here in our town before we moved here, it's something that is very rare. It doesn't happen often, and it probably will never happen here in this town again. The boy in the photos was seven years old and he was selling magazine subscriptions for the Cub Scouts. He knocked on someone's door and a man let him in and killed him. Then he drove up to Harriman State Park in New York and tried to hide his body. When the police were searching for him in the neighborhood and questioned him, he confessed to murdering the boy. His pants were gone because he sexually assaulted him." Silence followed Clark's father's description of the murder. Clark didn't completely understand what his father meant by the words "sexually assaulted" but he knew it must have been something terrible - especially since there was so much blood on the boy's thighs and between his legs in the photographs.

"So, the man who did it, he admitted to it?" the younger Clark Westfield asked.

"Yes." Replied Clark's father, then silently waited for the next question.

"How did they find the boy's body if he hid it?" was the next question from young Clark.

"After he told the police what happened, he brought them to the spot and showed them." was his father's response. Several more seconds of silence followed, and Mr. Westfield could see his 8 year old son trying to make sense of the situation and understand how such a terrible thing could happen. "Clark, some people do terrible things, and some people can be very violent," his father added. "But it's important for you to understand that man is now in jail, and he can't hurt anybody." Just then Clark's mother appeared in the doorway of the room. The door from the family room to the kitchen was divided in the middle and each half could be opened and closed separately. The bottom half was closed, and Clark's mother appeared from the waist up.

"Hey boys! Do you want me to bring your plates in and you can eat while watching the game? Why is the sound off on the TV?" she asked innocuously.

"I was just asking dad about the pictures of the dead boy in the garage," Clark exclaimed. Part of him wanted his mother to know that he had learned about something that only grown-ups knew about.

"What dead boy?" asked Clark's mother, bewildered. "What is he talking about?"

"Clark knocked over the file box from the MacDougal case and all the case files from the Della Russo boy's murder were in there and he saw them," replied Clark's father in a tone that was purposely nonchalant to indicate to his mother not to escalate the shock and trauma of an 8-year-old seeing murder victim almost his own age.

"What?! Oh no..Clark, don't look at those photos! That's your dad's work business and you just shouldn't look at things that aren't yours if they don't belong to you," erupted Clark's mother with a surge of histrionic drama. "And why do you have those files?" She directed the question at Clark's father whose hopes of de-escalation were long dashed. "You can't just leave things around for your son to find – what are you thinking? He doesn't need to be looking at any of that stuff!"

"Mom, I knocked it over by accident when I was on my bike…" Clark tried to explain in the hopes his mother would not be upset, but even by age 8 he had learned that once she started yelling there was no calling it back. She continued to yell over the boy's words.

"I just don't understand how you could leave the case files there so your son could find them and now he has to see all that. What else have you got in the garage? What other items can you leave around the house to strategically traumatize your children?" As she persisted in her rant, Clark's father started to yell back as reason and rationale continued to fail and emotion took over. Clark watched the familiar interplay of his parents fighting and sat saying nothing as their voices grew louder and louder. In a predictable fashion, Clark's father got up from the couch and stormed upstairs. As his mother continued yelling at his father and followed him into the foyer Clark heard the door to their bedroom slam in the distance. He knew the routine all

too well. His father would stay in his room for the rest of the

afternoon and evening. His mother would burst in at random intervals

and they would continue their heated arguing. This would now go on

all night. Clark slipped out the back door and got back on his bicycle

in the garage. He could see Chris Ratti out on the street waiting for

him. As he turned to leave the garage the box of case files caught his

eye as it rested on the shelf. His father had said the guy was in

jail…but where and for how long? That was what happened on July 4th

1976, the day this adventure of Clark Westfield started.

****

****

July 3, 2016

Forty years later an older, weathered, and tired Clark Westfield

walked into the entrance of the newsroom at the paper he worked for.

His pace was slightly slower than normal. At 48 he had spent his adult

life working as a reporter and helping readers understand a world that

no longer existed. Since that day in 1976, Clark had gone to college

and reported on various beats – municipal, education, politics, the police desk - finally earning enough seniority to have an opinion column and write long term investigative pieces. His column allowed him to have a point of view on stories he was covering as well as anything happening in the nation or the world, he felt was important. His last contract with the paper had given him the journalistic equivalent of tenure – he couldn't be fired unless he grabbed someone's ass or breast or stopped turning in articles. In New Jersey, Clark was a legendary reporter and his name well known in power circles all over the state and even the country. While he had contributed major magazine pieces to all the big national news weeklies over the years - TIME, Newsweek, the New Yorker, - he had resisted the once frequent recruitment efforts by bigger more prominent papers. The New York Times had approached him on no less than four occasions with four different editors begging him to come work for them. Clark never let them quote him a salary figure, he knew he would refuse regardless of the money. It was a source of pride for him to be a lead reporter at a major regional daily paper. In a state like New Jersey, that meant being a voice to more than 8 million people and all the news a densely populated state would generate.

Plus, New Jersey was so close to New York City that most of the city's workforce lived there and commuted every day. New Jersey residents drove cars and rode trains and buses from the six northern counties to work in industries with national implications. Fashion, finance, music, television, entertainment, Broadway theater and the headquarters of many companies that relied on mid-western manufacturing. Decisions made in New Jersey were decisions that affected the rest of America. While New York City was seen by many as the greatest city in the world and the center of trade, industry, culture, and world politics, it was across the river in the Garden State where all those decision makers and leaders actually lived, slept, breathed and played. There was an "everyman's" street cred to working at the New Jersey Examiner, one that Clark wore as a chip on his shoulder, and he let no one challenge it.

But on July 4th 2016, his pace was slower than usual. The enthusiasm and love for his job had long vanished. Four years ago, Clark's mentor and editor, a journalistic superhero named Steve Miller, had been forced to retire. Everyone in the newsroom thought he had simply grown older and wanted to spend time with his grandchildren –

and that is what Steve Miller had told them. But Clark knew the real

story. The real story was that the paper had been purchased by a large

national media company who bought the paper, as they put it "as a

foundation for their digital journalistic brands" - or whatever the hell

that meant. The parent company sold digital advertising and ran

various online outlets and social media apps – that was their core

business and they had bought countless regional daily newspapers to

create a stranglehold on local advertising revenue in more than a dozen

states. Steve Miller was an even more old school reporter than Clark-

he had been in the White house press pool at the time of the Cuban

Missile Crisis and the Kennedy assassination. He had gone abroad to

Vietnam with a local national guard regimen. By the time Watergate

unfolded Steve had become Managing Editor and no piece of news in

New Jersey was published without his edits and approval. Steve

Miller had been a great mentor to Clark, and he was also a confidant

and friend. Then one day four years ago, in November 2012, when

New Jersey was reeling from the chaos and destruction of Superstorm

Sandy, Steve had been called to New York City to meet with upper

management. Clark received a text from his editor and mentor that evening with the simple simple words "They won…" Then the next morning, at an all staff meeting in the newsroom Steve announced plans for his retirement to the staff. That evening the two men had gone out to their favorite diner – the Tick Tock diner on Rt. 3 – where Steve had told Clark he had recommended him to take his place as managing editor. It was a cathartic and wonderful evening. Becoming managing editor was everything Clark had ever dreamed of and while he would miss his friend and boss immensely, it was the highest career aspiration that still held any meaning to him. After a few tears and a hug, Clark went home that night to tell his wife that with Steve Miller leaving he was about to get a promotion.

But weeks went by, and no one said anything further. No one from management called him for a meeting or even to talk to him. Steve Miller said on more than one occasion he didn't know why it was taking so long or what the delay was. Then on another day four years ago, Clark walked into the newsroom at his usual morning arrival time to find three men in suits he didn't recognize and the rest of the staff gathered around. They were from corporate, and they ran the company that had bought the paper. Clark stood in silence as the older balding man told the staff how proud he was of the great work they were doing and how great they thought the newspaper was. Then he told the staff that it gave him great pleasure to announce the new managing editor would be Sean Caldwell. Clark stood in stunned silence as the smiling Caldwell moved to the center of the room and started talking about how flattered he was and his plans for the paper in the digital age. As he spoke Clark's cell phone buzzed with a text from Steve Miller. "I had no idea man. They didn't tell me anything." was all it said. It didn't have to say anymore. Clark was not and would never be managing editor.

But the problem wasn't just that Clark didn't get the job. The bigger problem was that he and Sean Caldwell hated each other's guts on deep visceral level and Caldwell was now Clark's new boss. Since that day, Clark's pace as he entered the building from the parking lot was slightly slower. So slow in fact that one day he knew it was going to slow to a complete stop, and he would simply turn around, walk back to his car and drive home never to return. The only reason that day wasn't today was because he didn't have a plan for what he would do when he got home. As he moved one heavy foot in front of the other, he wondered what would come first – would he plan some brilliant next career move in middle age or simply go home in disgust and turn on the television… "Just keep moving forward," he told himself.

The morning editorial meeting was at 10 AM each day and section editors and reporters would sit and reveal what they were working on in their various departments. That morning Clark sat there and said nothing as the section heads reported on what was in store for the next day's paper. Usually, Clark listened and then would scour the national headlines before deciding on an opinion piece. But this morning Sean Caldwell zeroed in on him.

"Westfield, what are you working on today?" he asked in a short, curt tone.

"Umm…I was going to solve peace in the middle east and then cure cancer.." replied Clark smartly as the room met him with laughter. Junior reporters loved his acerbic wit and confident posture.

"Great wise ass, when you are finished, I want you to go interview MacDougal," shot Caldwell.

"I'm sorry? Who?"

"Joseph MacDougal, the child murderer you interviewed 25 years ago," replied Caldwell.

Despite pleading guilty to the murder of the 7-year-old Della Russo boy, Joseph MacDougal had been sentenced to 25 years to life in prison, and was first eligible for parole after 13 years. At the time of his first parole hearing no one thought it was realistic he would be released given the heinous crime and public outrage from the murder. But the second time he became eligible was after he had served 16 years, and that time it looked like he might be paroled after all. That was in the early 1990's and and a rookie reporter just out of journalism school, Clark was covering the campaign by the victim's parents and family to make sure he stayed in prison. It was a lengthy community advocacy story and Clark had interviewed the boy's parents, friends, pastor, teachers. Finally, he interviewed Joseph MacDougal in prison in Trenton. To this day, Clark was the only reporter MacDougal had ever spoken to.

"Why do you want me to interview Joseph MacDougal? I already interviewed him back in the early 90's. I'll pull the article for you if you want…" replied Clark confrontationally. Suddenly the big conference room full of his colleague reporters felt very claustrophobic…

"Because you are the only guy he will talk to, Westfield," replied Sean Caldwell. "I can't imagine you being the only guy ANYONE wants to speak to, though this is a rather odious character." Caldwell glanced around the table in an attempt to harvest laughs from the lackeys.

"And why the hell do you want me to interview that murderous scumbag again?" interrupted Clark.

"Westfield….." sighed the editor. "He's up for parole again. You're the only guy that can do this."

Clark felt a lump in his throat as he suddenly felt the sickness in his stomach from that day back in the garage. He swallowed hard and tried to get the images of the seven-year-old cub scouts pant-less, bloodied legs and swollen face out of his mind.

"Guess I'm off to Trenton…" Clark shrugged and left the conference room….

Chapter 2

Clark pulled into the driveway of the Metuchen house and turned off the car ignition and the radio. He sighed. In all his years as a reporter, the Della Russo murder had always haunted him. The box of legal files he had accidentally knocked over as a kid in his family's home garage had unwillingly forced a tutorial on the details of a brutal and violent act of rage against a child. And it happened right in their hometown a few years before Clark's family had moved there. Clark's father, Clark Westfield Senior, was in his first year out of law school, working as an attorney and happened to be working at a prominent county law firm when a seven-year-old boy had been murdered. The boy had disappeared selling magazine subscriptions for his scout troop and the town had launched a frantic weekend long search. Ultimately the police narrowed it down to a certain house where he was last seen and questioned the occupant, a junior college history teacher. During the police interrogation at the man's house, he had suddenly asked to see a priest and the police obliged, assuming he wanted to confess to the crime, perhaps first to clergy. A local parish priest was summoned and permitted to spend time alone with the suspect. Upon emerging from the house, the priest walked up to the police car and said simply "He did it. He wants to show you guys where he is."

And just like that the police and the town had their answers, horrible as they were. Joseph MacDougal told the police he had killed the boy, and Clark's father had gotten the call in the middle of dinner that his law firm would be taking the case. Also in that night's phone call was a directive from the owner of the law firm that Clark's father was to accompany the police, detectives, prosecutor's office investigators and the murderer himself to the site where he had hidden the boy's body. And also, just like that, Clark's father looked at the family gathered around the dinner table with a sickened look and simply said "I've got to go now…don't wait up for me." Clark's mother had no idea where her husband was going at that moment when he rose from the table and slowly put on his coat and hat. But she knew she had never seen that look on him before. It wasn't fear. It was more of a deep despair, like he knew what he was about to see and that he didn't want to but had to go through with it.

The killer had hidden the boy's body in Harriman State Park, a beautiful huge tract of land that used to belong to a mining company in the 1800's. The Harriman family had leased huge tracts of wilderness to various mining companies for copper, zinc, silver, bauxite - anything but coal. That local industry and regional dynamics it created were of enormous interest to a history professor and MacDougal had familiarize himself with dozens of the various mines that had been dug out and abandoned in what was now a state park. So, when it came time for him to hide the body of a little boy he had just killed, that was where he went. And that was where Clark's father went that night – into a mine in Harriman State Park to make sure that his client and the chain of evidence he was about to expose was handled properly. The police took photos of the area and of course the boy's body. They then formally charged the teacher with the murder and performed an autopsy, determining that he had been killed by blunt force trauma to the head and also been sexually assaulted. Then three years later, young Clark learned all these details when the case files had spilled all over his garage. Clark's father had filled him in the on rest, along with existential reassurances that while bad things happened in the world the little boy would always be safe. The experience had deeply and permanently affected Clark.

As time went on and Clark had gotten older, he would ask his father additional details about the case. The young boy's family had made a grand and appropriate effort to memorialize him, with a statue dedicated to him outside the local church – the same church where the priest served that had gotten his murderer to confess. His mother and father had given countless media interviews about how wonderful and full of life he was. His school portrait was embedded in the shrine statue outside the church. In fact, the timeline and details of the case were so tidy that if Norman Rockwell had to paint the unfortunate portrait of a small-town community struggling its way through a child's murder, he simply could have painted a scene from anywhere on the timeline. But something about it didn't add up. The murdered boy was hard to forget – so hard to forget that Clark had lived with a nagging obsession as to why anyone on earth could ever be capable of purposely hurting such an icon of innocence. In Clark's high school psychology class, he read about compulsion and learned what a sociopath was. It was then at age 17 that he had asked his father to tell him where the case files were so he could read them again as a more mature adolescent. Clark's father had the sense to discourage him from reading any of the files and told him any attention paid to such a terrible event was time wasted that would sour his mood and he would never get that time back. But nothing in a house escapes the deliberate scrutiny of a 17-year-old boy. When Clark eventually found the file boxes that had been hidden in the attic, he simply didn't tell his father.

Clark read them and re-read them, as gruesome as they were. With each read of the legal brief and scouring of the autopsy photos, his fascination with the killer's motive grew. What could possibly deteriorate in a person's psyche to make them that dangerous – that angry? Then when Clark was in college, Joseph MacDougal became eligible for parole. It seemed absurd that someone who had plead guilty to such a brutal act would have the possibility of walking free – but sure enough the guilty plea was for aggravated manslaughter which carried a 25 year to life term. That meant he would be eligible for parole in 13 years. The first time he was eligible, in 1988, the parole board didn't even hear the case and there was no news. However, the next time – four years later – there was in fact going to be a hearing scheduled. In advance of the hearing, the little Della Russo boy's parents lead a local community advocacy movement to call attention to the possibility this brutal killer could walk free. They encouraged letter writing campaigns, which they had no problem gathering. They held a vigil outside the Catholic Church at the shrine. They went on television and had to plead their case all over again in the hopes they didn't watch any last shred of justice for their son evaporate into thin air. That was Clark's first year working at the paper. He was a college intern.

When Clark had walked into that morning's news assignment meeting the legendary editor Steve Miller was giving out assignments surrounding the parole hearing. Several of the reporters in that meeting had covered the boy's disappearance, the location of his body, his confession and each and every interval of the trial and sentencing over the next 14 months. When the meeting ended and the room cleared, Clark took Steve Miller aside and asked simply whether he could have an interview with Joseph MacDougal while he was behind bars in Trenton State Penitentiary. Instead of belittling an eager intern who appeared to be punching above his weight, Steve Miller looked at him and gently replied that MacDougal would never talk to a reporter, to which Clark replied "We'll see, I may have an in with the guy…"

Whether that was naivete or bravado depends on your point of view, but that meeting had ended with the editor slapping Clark on his back and saying "I admire your temerity, kid" while chuckling. But words instructing Clark NOT to seek an interview were never spoken. And just like that, young 22-year-old Clark Westfield had set out to Trenton with the intention of getting a sit down interview with Joseph MacDougal, a popular college teacher who had raped and murdered a seven year old boy who was selling magazine subscriptions.

What Clark didn't tell his editor at the time was that he planned on using the letter of appearance he had swiped from the case files in his home to get an appointment with the murderer. Clark and his father had the same name, which was a source of both pride and confusion. This time it was his ticket into prison. What he also hadn't told his editor was that he had already filed a meeting request with the prison warden, complete with a copy of the appearance letter on the law firm's letterhead. They were expecting him, and with MacDougal coming up for parole a meeting with his defense attorney would be seen as routine. The only thing that could foil Clark's plan was that he looked young - perhaps too young to have graduated law school. But would they care? It was worth a shot.

Upon arriving at the intake office on the prison grounds, a greying, near retirement age prison guard who held a clipboard simply held out his hand to take Clark's ID, then screened down a list on the clipboard he was holding, found the line where the names matched, wrote the arrival time in the margin column, handed Clark back his ID and waved him through barely without even glancing up. No words spoken, just an indifferent wave. The corrections officers in charge of visitation and inmate/attorney conferences led Clark to a small room with pale green paint and a steel table in the middle. Five minutes later the electronic lock on the door buzzed and Joseph MacDougal walked in. The tall and lanky man with a gleaming streak of sweat in the groves of his forehead walked slowly across the room with his eyes on Clark and sat down. They sat in silence for several moments before Clark spoke first.

"Hello..uh…Mr. MacDougal, I'm a reporter with the Newark Examiner and I'd like to interview you with your parole hearing coming up," was the first thing that Clark could think to say.

MacDougal smiled and said "I thought it was unusual that my lawyer would want to see me. You've got balls kid… now go fuck yourself." And he rose from the chair to leave. Clark, in an effort not to lose the interview blurted out:

"My father was your attorney!" Clark blurted out. "He and I have the same name. I'm sorry but I'm a reporter and I think it's important you tell your story, so I used the family connection to try to arrange an interview with you. If you really don't want to do this, fine. I'll leave. But with your parole hearing coming up I would think you'd want your side out there on the record."

"Oh? And what side is that?" asked MacDougal with an intense stare. "The side where I described how I killed him, and you get your big interview? Coming in here on the coattails of your father and trying to make a name for yourself? I don't have a shot at parole – you know that, and I know that so what's the point?"

"Well…I think a lot of people want to know…at least I certainly want to know…. "

"You and everyone else want to know why, right? You want to know why I killed him right? What did your father tell you about the case?" growled MacDougal.

"Uh..well.." Clark stammered, "I've read the case files, and all the news coverage…"

"The newspapers don't know jack shit," the killer shouted. "They make shit up – the same way you're going to after this interview."

"Well then let's discuss what the newspapers got wrong," pressed Clark. "What is it that you want people to know that wasn't reported correctly?"

"Did your father tell you what happened when they found him?" MacDougal shot back.

"Umm.. no…he didn't like to talk about it much. I saw the pictures but.."

"Yeah, even your good old dad couldn't handle the truth…" MacDougal cocked his head back and laughed maniacally. "Nobody will ever fucking believe me….they think I just killed him and that's the end of it….geez…" MacDougal looked him dead in the eyes. "Son, you don't need an interview with me. Everything you need to put in that paper is up there where they found him."

"What do you mean? You mean up in Harriman State Park?" asked Clark somewhat bewildered but aware he may be trying to follow the manipulations of a madman.

"You go find the mine…it's all up there in the mine. Then we'll talk." And with that Joseph MacDougal rose from his chair and knocked on the door to be let out. That was April 8, 1992.

When Clark got back to the newsroom after his first visit to the prison, he told Steve Miller what had happened including the phony appearance letter he had used to gain access to the prison and arrange the interview. Steve Miller smiled behind his old wise eyes and said simply:

"You're going to make a great reporter kid – not because of what you did but because you had enough sense not to tell me how you were going to do it – the same way I never told you not to. You and I can work together. As it stands now, even though you're an intern, you're the only staffer here that got an interview with him on the record. I know he didn't tell you much but it's safe to say he is defiant before his parole hearing and that's what you'll write. But you better learn something from this and it's not about phony letters and surname shell games – those are the tools of our trade which frankly anyone can learn, and you already know. What you MUST learn on this job is that there are people as fucked up and crazy as MacDougal in this world and you cannot not let them in your head to wreak havoc – because believe me – they will."

His editor then assigned Clark some of the periphery reporting with the Della Russo boy's parents, the police and other relevant connections. Clark got a hell of alot more than he bargained for as he heard their grief, anguish and horror firsthand. Then Clark's newspaper ran an article that was displayed as a full-length interview with the killer with some minor quotes and heavy "observational filler" that basically said the killer had no remorse before his first parole hearing. And while that wasn't precisely true, as that hadn't really come up in their very brief interaction – there were no actual lies in the coverage either. The story ran and Clark won his first journalism award that year as a rookie, under the watchful eye and wise tutelage of Steve Miller. Then Clark graduated and was hired as a full time beat reporter with investigative assignments, went on to other stories and tried and hoped to never think about the Della Russo boy and Joseph MacDougal ever again.

But here he was on the fourth of July weekend in 2016 being told by an editor who knew nothing about the original circumstances that he had to go and attempt another interview. No one knew what happened in that prison conference room that day other than Joseph MacDougal, Clark Westfield and Steve Miller. Clark always carried some guilt deep down that the story that had put him on the map, gotten the attention of the paper's editor, and earned him a mentor had knowingly been presented on false pretenses. Even after all this time, it nagged him and gave him imposter syndrome every time he thought about the case. He had compensated for it over the years with major full-length interviews of very important and newsworthy people and as the years went on he eventually achieved genuine journalistic greatness. But only Clark knew where it all had started and could never forget MacDougal's demeanor and the conviction in his voice about "what really happened." It always ate at him at some level. He just never had the guts to revisit it.

As he sat in his driveway in his car with the ignition off, this is what was on his mind. Clark walked up the stone path in the front yard into his house. His gait was heavy and burdened. As he walked through the threshold and his eyes adjusted to the dimmer light inside, he could smell something glorious cooking and through the steam and sounds of searing coming from the kitchen, his wife turned around and waved.

"Hi! Dinner will be ready in a few minutes, but I can't stay – I have to meet the boys," said his wife in her cheery tone. She was always in an upbeat mood. "What is the matter with you? You look like you are carrying ten sandbags on your shoulders."

"Mare it's been a tough day.." said Clark in a low dejected voice. His wife, Mary Lynn, was a strong, kind woman. They had been married more than 25 years and while they had all the dents and scratches that come with so many years of marriage, they still loved one another unwaveringly and had raised three children together. Clark had coined the term "battlefield nuptials" as a way of acknowledging what all couples know to be true - that no marriage is free from conflict. Clark had learned long ago that while he and Mary

Lynn had vast differences in their personalities and their interests, they cared for one another at a very deep level. And although he didn't understand all of her work as a psychotherapist and she didn't understand all of the tedious work of investigative journalism, there was a familiarity with the fundamentals of each other's characters and true nature that he simply didn't share with any other person. There was no fooling one another on the basics no matter how busy life got or how challenging marriage could be. Clark and Mary Lynn knew one another. And for this Clark harbored enormous gratitude..

"I've got five minutes….what was so tough about today?" she asked and sat down next to him and leaned on him affectionately.

"Fucking Caldwell wants me to go interview Joseph MacDougal – that dirtbag is coming up for parole again," he replied.

"Ohh… that's such a horrible story…." reflected by Mary Lynn Westfield. "But you've interviewed him before and who better to put this in perspective for the public than Clark Westfield? Few people know as much about the case as you do – nobody can describe its historical significance like you, Clark. What is it that is really bothering you – is it just dwelling on all the horrible details again?"

"Well Mare, it's complicated," Clark sighed and took a deep breath. "The whole thing is just so upsetting. From the first day when I saw the case files.."

"I know – we've talked about this one hundred times," his wife interrupted. "You were a young boy and you saw a boy's murdered body and you never forgot it. But you interviewed him when you were starting out and that showed everybody how damn good a reporter you were and…"

"Well, it didn't exactly go down like that…" Clark cut her off. "I interviewed him, yes, but it was short, and I didn't really get much of an interview. He yelled at me, told me that my father didn't have the guts to tell me the truth and that I should go to the site where they found the body. I just figured he was such a scumbag that if the paper ran an interview story implying, he wasn't contrite it was close enough to the truth that I could still sleep at night. Plus, I loved having him on the record with no remorse because I saw what he did to that boy, and I saw what that monster was capable of… I needed to make sure the public and parole board understood that."

"Right-so now you have to do that again. I don't think there is a chance in hell that he is going to get parole – there would be too much outrage. Plus, I doubt he will talk to you again – what's in it for him? Why don't you make a request for the interview and let him decline, then assign the retrospective coverage to a junior reporter and you're done! Walk away!" Mary Lynn Westfield smiled a warm encouraging smile that normally would have disarmed Clark and calmed him down. "Is it that you feel guilty about the first interview? That it was too short? You didn't lie Clark...."

"I went in there under false pretenses," Clark shot back. "I impersonated my father and got in a room with the guy because I had to see him for myself. I wasn't cleverly orchestrating my big break; it was way more selfish than that. The 8-year-old boy that is still inside had to see what kind of person could do such a thing. It was almost like until I saw him with my own eyes, I couldn't believe a person like that was real.   My editor set it up like I had a big sit-down interview with him and I let it all happen."

"And it put you on the map – it made your editor want to mentor you – it put you on the crime desk for a while – It was your big break –

what is it that bothers you so much Clark? Steve Miller didn't mentor you because of your terrifically short interview, he mentored you because you were clever enough to find your way into that prison and sit across from an extremely dangerous and secretive man. You did that and climbed over the shoulders of a dozen reporters in Steve Miller's newsroom who also had that assignment and couldn't make it happen. People don't invest in you because they learn what you are thinking, they invest in you because of what they see you do. Life's big breaks are never as majestic as they seem from the outside." She was being persuasively reassuring.

"There was something about him…" Clark spoke slowly. "There was something about his demeanor and his confidence that day that I couldn't put my finger on. Then he kept telling me to go to the spot in Harriman – up to that damn mine – implying that there was something newsworthy there…I never told anyone that part."

"Well, he was a killer who had murdered a child," said Mary Lynn gently. "You weren't interviewing Martha Stewart; you were interviewing a violent manipulative sociopath – I'd worry if you weren't uncomfortable after that interview. Did you ever go up to the park and check out the mine?"

"I've been in that park hundreds of times. I've hiked most of the trails, swam in the different lakes, but I never went to the exact spot. I didn't see the point," explained Clark. "I didn't want that creep to send me on a wild goose chase and succeed in further manipulation. These fuckers love toying with your head. Every time my dad would take me to that state park it was so beautiful – gorgeous rock formations, gorgeous birds and wildlife. But it was always in the back of my mind that this was where he had hidden that little boy's body, and my dad always mentioned it at some point in the hike or the picnic."

"I think you are overthinking this," his wife said. "First of all, you don't know if he will even grant you the interview – he most likely won't and it will be over. Do your due diligence. Put in the request as you were assigned and take everything one step at a time. You've interviewed plenty of bad people and other murderers."

"Yeah….," said Clark in a low voice. "But this one was different…."

The next morning Clark got up as the sun came up. He hadn't slept well. His wife Mary Lynn rolled over in visible displeasure at the noise he made. July mornings were still hot – as if the sun hadn't set at all. Prior to going to sleep the night before, Clark had written an email to the Bureau of Corrections requesting an interview with the prisoner Joseph MacDougal. Clark was in their system as a credentialed reporter, and he had done many interviews at the various state prisons throughout his career – so the days of impersonating his father were long gone. In fact, that had only happened that one time. But none of his other requests over the years had been for MacDougal. They had all been for other newsworthy prisoners who had no idea who Clark was unless they had read his articles. He was eager to check his email and see a denial response and then, like his wife said, "it would all be over." But as he scrolled through the advertisement, solicitation and story pitches from clueless publicists, he realized it was unrealistic to get a response this early in the morning on a Saturday. He lazily made his way into the basement of the Westfield family home - towards a box in the corner that was taped shut with brown masking tape. The cardboard was worn and soggy. The lid was floppy and damp with age. It smelled like old wet dirt.

The box contained the case files found in Clark's garage so many years ago. After his father had passed away, Clark had found them in the attic of his home and made a decision not to throw them away. His father had taken the file box the day Clark had knocked them over in the garage; he had seen them again at age 17. The next time he saw them was some years ago as they were cleaning out his parent's estate for sale. He could never bring himself to either open it or throw it out after that second examination– and it occurred to him he didn't even know what was still in there – he just recognized the box. With shaky hands he lifted the lid and musty smell and dust raised up into his nose and eyes. He coughed and squinted and looked inside. There were old papers, and he could see the yellowing oak tag backing with the word "Kodak" printed on it. See The dreadful photos were still there – yellowed and still out of order from the day Clark had knocked them over. He didn't need to look at them again – but there was one in particular he was looking for. The discussion with his wife had gotten him thinking about MacDougal's cackling laughter so many years ago and his yelling at ear splitting volume to "Look in the mine!!" Clark

had lay awake all night wondering what he possibly could have meant

and come to the conclusion that he simply must know, or he would

never escape the tormenting echoes in his brain. Plus, there was this

piece of him that intuitively felt he was going to wind up sitting down

with that murderer again at some point and he would have to answer

the question as to whether he had in fact done as he had been

instructed. At first that seemed absurd, but not when you include the

accountability Clark felt to this Joseph MacDougal was partly to offset

this lingering sense of guilt. MacDougal was the only living person on

the planet who knew what had happened in that interview room all

those years back and it made Clark very anxious in a way he couldn't

describe. Clark had always known there would come a day when he

would go up to the mine once when he knew what he would be

looking for. And it seemed that time was now, but Clark didn't have a

clue what he should be looking for after more than 40 years.

He side glanced each photograph taking a quick peek and turning

them over if they were an autopsy photo of a wound or other

anatomical detail. He flipped the best he could to avoid seeing the brutality in the decade's old pictures. Some had started to crack, and the chemicals used in developing the photos caused chips to fall off leaving wide spaces where the picture had vanished, and the white backing of the photo paper shown through. Finally, he found the one he was looking for that he remembered so well. It was a wide shot of several people in the woods, perhaps a dozen men who seemed to be the investigation team. At different perspectives in the photo the men were in various stages of ascending a rocky trail. There were steep rock walls on each side. Half of the men in the photo were in uniform – he could distinguish several different municipal police uniforms and several park rangers. One man in plain clothes had a shirt and tie and a badge hung on a chain around his neck, a gun holster clearly visible around his waist. He must have been a detective. Many of the men wore mustaches, a common trend in the early 1970's, especially in law enforcement. In the corner of the photograph a man's arm and shoulder were in the frame but not the rest of him. That man could have been Clark's father… and Clark liked the idea that there was his dad on the job – keeping watch to make sure the police collected evidence and tagged it appropriately. At the upper end of the rocky path in the photo was what looked like the mouth of a huge cave. It was at least 20 feet high, as far as he could tell, and seemed to disappear into total blackness. One man seemed to be standing slightly inside the mouth of the cave and was wearing a helmet with a light on it – a miner's helmet – and pointing towards the back. Clark figured this must be the spot that MacDougal had led them to, and the man was pointing to something significant. Clark turned over the photograph to look at the back and there in faded pencil were the words "Bradley Mine – Location of Cadaver" Bingo! But how would Clark find this Bradley Mine? Harriman State Park was almost 50,000 acres, only a fraction of which were accessible by trails, let alone roads. It was the largest park in New York State and covered more than 4 counties.

Clark went upstairs to find his 19-year-old daughter Melody sitting at the kitchen counter eating a bowl of cereal. He could hear the music blasting out of her headphones from across the living room. He walked up behind her talking only to realize she couldn't hear him at all, so he tapped her on the shoulder. She jumped as if given an electric shock.

"DAD!" she gasped. "What the hell! You scared the hell out of me!"

"Well, I didn't exactly sneak up on you – I was talking to you across the whole room!" Clark laughed. He could tell that she was up early to go out for a run as she was dressed in skintight yoga pants with a sweatband around her head.

"Why are you up so early? It's Saturday and you don't jog…as far as I know…unless you had a mid-life crisis in the middle of the night and want to join me," Melody giggled. Clark and his daughter teased each other all the time and it was a sign of the mutual affection in their relationship.

"Well, I had to do some research and I hit a dead end. Can I have some coffee?" Clark helped himself to the pot of coffee Melody had made for herself.

"Sure dad – but that's decaf." Melody said as she grabbed his hand which was holding the photograph, he had examined downstairs.

"Decaf??? Why the hell would anyone EVER make decaf coffee?? That is like wearing a raincoat in the shower! You'd never make it in a newsroom Melody." Clark teased and poured the coffee down the drain.

"Yeah whatever – let's see how your colon and heart tolerate your full-strength caffeinated beverages in 20 years. What is this a picture of?" asked his daughter as she turned over the photo in Clark's hand. "Bradley Mine…what is Bradley Mine?"

"Oh this…umm…it's an old file photo of a VERY old case…wait do you know Bradley mine? Have you ever heard of it?" asked Clark.

"Well, no but why don't you just google it? I'm sure you can find it pretty easy…" as Melody was talking she opened her phone which was secured to her arm with an elastic exercise band and started typing in the search engine. Clark just stood there, watching. The fact that the younger generation had the entire planet's worth of knowledge at their fingertips in a phone and had immediate access to things that took Clark years to find in the old days never ceased to amaze him. "Here it is!" She handed Clark her phone. As he scrolled through the page she had found she took the phone back and read out loud "Bradley Mine is one of dozens of abandoned iron mines in Harriman State Park

with a "walk in " entrance. It is accessible by a trail but in a restricted area of the park and off limits to hikers. People are discouraged from finding or visiting the mine because of the hazards that surround it. There you go. And here is a little map with pictures. Whoever made this blog entry clearly visited it when they weren't supposed to."
Clark thought for a moment.

"Were you going to go for a run right now?" he asked Melody. She nodded in agreement. "OK You want some exercise? You wanna go find that mine with me instead?"

Melody's eyes lit up with childlike excitement.

"I don't know dad; can you keep up with me?"

And off they went to find the mine….

Chapter 3

Elizabeth Cranford let her eyes adjust to the brightly lit newsroom as the sunrise blasted shards of orange and yellow over the Newark skyline. She stood at the massive wall sized glass windows and momentarily forgot about the beads of sweat slowly inching down her spine under her sports bra. She had just finished her morning run in the July heat and wanted to catch her breath and let her heart rate and blood pressure return to normal. There hadn't been a new skyscraper built in Newark since the early 1970's. From where Elizabeth was standing, she could see the classic mid-century architecture that dominated the shops and office buildings. The immense stone skyscraper which was the old Broad National Bank building on the corner of Broad and Market streets had once been the tallest building in New Jersey – though nowhere near as tall as some of the gargantuan monoliths across the river in Manhattan, which were visible through the windows perpendicular to where Elizabeth stood. There were new buildings and town houses that dotted empty lots with fresh

coats of paint. The Prudential Arena, which the New Jersey

Devils professional hockey team called home, rose up as an

obstruction on Mulberry Street. The controversial sports arena

hosted athletics and events which were of no real interest or use

to the people who actually lived in Newark, and growing up

Elizabeth didn't even know that New Jersey had a hockey team.

The social segregation in cultural pillars like sports and music

persisted to this day. Elizabeth Cranford was an African

American woman in her 30's, born and raised in the height of the

strife of the 1980's crack epidemic that had made Newark a

virtual war zone. A brilliant student with the heart of a lion,

Elizabeth held her head high and managed to use the lessons

learned, resilience and raw compassion of her poverty stricken

black family and thrive in a world dominated by middle class

white men who looked at her with pity, or perhaps worse - a

problem to be solved and an opportunity to absolve their classist

guilt. They disgusted her but she gave them the embellished

praise their social archetypes were expecting - all the time. In turn she told herself she was paying the rent for her family's apartment, grocery bills, and health insurance. She was the first in her family to go to college, which Steve Miller had arranged by encouraging her to apply for the newspaper's journalism scholarship and making her his intern. She studied with a vengeance, completing two advanced post graduate degrees at Rutgers right there in town. She had interned at the paper for her entire undergraduate journalism program after then editor Steve Miller recruited her out of one of his classes. Clark had guest lectured several of Steve Miller's journalism classes and Elizabeth had stood out as smart and challenging. So, Steve put her to work under Clark, first as a copy editor back before grammar and spell check made everyone's lives easier. Over the years she had grown into one of the paper's most talented and respected writers, taken assignments in just about every department and won several awards.

And as she stood high above the city, she knew more than anyone what was under the cosmetic façade her very paper had labeled an "urban renaissance." She had grown up listening to her parents tell stories of police beatings in a time when being born into the working class in Newark also meant dying there for a black person. At her very dinner table, she had heard a thousand times about how the national guard had sealed off the city in 1967 and weeks of rioting led to looting, curfews and countless deaths. As a child she grew up in the void created by crack and AIDS and turned her public housing development into hell on earth. With no hope of paying for college her parents kept up the encouragement and kept her on a tight leash while searching far and wide for scholarship opportunities. They found none but Elizabeth had applied to Rutgers anyway, and upon turning 18 qualified for student loans. She scraped up enough money from her job working at the airport transporting old people in wheelchairs to their gates to enroll in college. Steve Miller taught a news writing class in addition to his editorial role at the paper, and one day in an effort at constructive criticism, learned exactly how brilliant, tenacious and tough Elizabeth Cranford could be. It was after that first post class assignment showdown that he created an internship at the paper, told

Elizabeth to report for work the following Monday, and helped her fill out an application for a new scholarship at the paper no one seemed to have heard of. And just like that, her reporting career began. And after almost two decades of dogged beat reporting, fights with editors, lawyers, advertisers and sources, with all the awards she'd won and a reservoir of respect deeper than the city itself, Elizabeth stood there over the city she had conquered still feeling incomplete.

"Hey Cranford…Whatcha looking at?" rang the soft slimy voice of her now editor Sean Caldwell.

"Jesus…don't ever sneak up on me like that," she stepped away from her editor who had silently moved into her personal space in an attempt to surprise her as a practical joke.

"Sorry – I couldn't resist," he chortled. "Did I ever tell you that I love the fact that you are the first one in the newsroom every morning? Since you are here, come on in my office, I have a new assignment I want you to handle." Elizabeth felt her reflective moment slip away and the momentum of the day started. Like most reporters, she found silence deafening and a story assignment represented a plan for the day, a goal, the security of purpose.

"What do you know about the Della Russo murder case?" asked Caldwell as he adjusted his pretentious, initialed cufflinks. Elizabeth thought for a moment. She knew every detail of the case because she had researched it as Clark's subordinate, but he always cut off conversations about the case when she brought it up.

"Well, I know the facts and the chronology of the case from our archives. It happened more than 10 years before I was born. I know the perp is coming up for parole again and the poor boy's family is going to have to mount a publicity campaign to keep the dirt bag who murdered him behind bars. Why do you ask – I sense an assignment coming." Elizabeth smiled, hoping to be given a story related to the murder.

"Yeah well, you're right," replied her editor. He paused to sip his coffee. "You were in the board meeting yesterday morning and you heard me say we were going to devote some coverage to the upcoming parole hearing."

"Yeah, and you assigned Clark Westfield an interview with the killer in prison because he interviewed him before," interrupted Elizabeth.

"Yes, I did," Caldwell nodded. "And that's all I need from him. The rest is going to have to come from you."

"The rest?" asked Elizabeth.

"Yeah, the rest," Caldwell took another gulp of coffee. "There are a ton of additional angles we are going to have to sort through. The boy's mother is still alive, there has been legislation passed in response to the murder, there is an FBI profiler who did a deep study of the perp.."

"Why wouldn't Clark do those things if he is going to handle the main story?" Elizabeth was genuinely inquisitive and didn't understand why her editor would bifurcate the assignments.

"Well frankly…and this is just you and me talking here, right?" Caldwell gave her a look that implied he was seeking her confidence regarding whatever was about to come out of his mouth next. Elizabeth shrugged and nodded. "Well Liz, frankly

I'm not sure Clark is up to the task, and I need some insurance that we are going to get what we need for the coverage we want so you're my ringer."

"What do you mean you don't think Clark is up to it? I certainly can't get an interview with MacDougal – only Clark can do that. Plus, I don't know what you are talking about with Clark not being up to it – he is one of the best if not the best reporter I've ever met, and you know he'll get the job done. Also, he has been reporting on this case for decades - he knows all those sources you just mentioned by first name! What is this really about Sean?" asked Elizabeth.

"Oh really?" Caldwell shot back. He had uncanny energy for so early in the morning. "And what happened with that big opioid story you guys worked on last summer? Huh? What did Clark turn in? What did he actually DO at all?"

"Clark did a ton on that story! If it wasn't for him.." Elizabeth stammered.

"What? Wasn't it for him what? You do realize that he didn't turn in one byline after his flowery obituary, and you turned in several week's worth of great reporting AND you flipped a drug rep. He followed you around for weeks pretending to be on some scoop while you did all the work! I know he hired you out of college and all, but you are simply too kind a woman to see what's really going on here." Caldwell slowed down his speech and talked in a lower voice. "Liz, I have to assign Clark the prison interview with MacDougal. I don't have a choice on that. But anything else that can be done by someone else will be. I want you to go with Clark when he interviews MacDougal. I want you to make sure it gets done. And I want you to share a by line." Elizabeth looked at her editor and fought feelings of pride, contempt and duplicitousness. She would have LOVED to do the prison interview, but she categorically disagreed with Sean Caldwell's assertion that her old mentor and boss was washed up or in any way compromised.

"Sean," Elizabeth began to choose her words carefully. "I'd love to work on this story. I'd love to help in an interview with the murderer if it's needed. But I'm not going to interfere with a story that Clark started on more than 25 years ago and I absolutely disagree with your implication that he is not up to any task. You don't really know Clark and he did an enormous amount of work last summer on that opioid story – work that you'll never understand. I'm uncomfortable even talking about a colleague's performance with you. It's inappropriate."

"Inappropriate? Seriously?" Caldwell looked at her mockingly. "That's your generation's label for anything that's hard in life..'inappropriate' everything that's uncomfortable or causes you to cringe, you millennials throw out the word 'inappropriate' like it's some kind of social panic button. Well, I got news for you Liz…and the quicker you learn this the better – LIFE is inappropriate. Life is messy. Life isn't fair. Life eats people alive- especially once great people like your buddy Clark. Plus, it's time for you to shine and get out from under his shadow."

"I'm sorry?" Elizabeth didn't know what to make of the discussion her editor was instigating.

"Let's face it. How much time does he really have left here? He is at the top of his pay grade; he turns in a couple columns each week which frankly are the musings of an old man – granted he still has some readers out there which is what keeps his paycheck coming but you and I both know it's twilight for Clark Westfield and has been for some time." Caldwell's facial expression was accompanied by the nodding of his head the way someone accents their speech and movements when they are being persuasive and want you to agree with them.

"Sean don't play me like this and leave me out of it ok?" Elizabeth was now acutely bothered. "I ain't got time for this."

"You're right, I'm sorry. It's my problem as editor to deal with staff issues…and I will," he turned to face her with a transparently insincere smile. "You'll learn all this when you have your own bureau to look after. I'm planning on making you city editor." Sean Caldwell turned to the full-length windows and pointed to the Newark skyline. "Look out there Liz – that's the city that you grew up in and conquered. You deserve to run a metro newsroom – hell Newark is accountable to Elizabeth

Cranford! It might be three months – could be six – but the new owners are going to announce some structural changes here and I just thought you should know I plan on promoting you."

Elizabeth stood stunned not knowing what to say…

"Well…ummm," she stammered.

"Is that millennial for thank you?" asked Sean with a devilish grin.

"I'm flattered…," Elizabeth managed to whisper under her breath. She turned and walked out of the office. And just like that, Elizabeth Cranford learned that she was going to be newspaper editor for the city in which she grew up and defied all socio-economic odds. And as the elevator doors shut, she frantically tapped a text to Clark Westfield. "Call me ASAP!!"

****

*****

Melody Westfield flipped through the radio stations on the center console of the car driven by her father. As they headed north on the Garden State Parkway passing Exit 135, she left the dial on the Beatles station and smiled at her dad.

"What's your favorite Beatles song dad?" she asked, smiling.

"Listen Mel, you know how much I love listening to the saints from Liverpool, but can you take out your tablet and let's read a little bit about where we are going." Clark asked his daughter kindly. "Can you look up Harriman State Park?" as Clark spoke his daughter turned down the radio and started a search on her tablet.

"So, it says here that Harriman State Park is in southern New York on the New Jersey border, it's over 47,000 acres and it's about 30 miles north of New York City."

"Keep reading," said Clark. "Who was it named after?"

"Umm…it says here that the park was named after a railroad tycoon named Edward Harriman who had this gigantic estate. Wow, that's all one person's property? What did Edward Harriman do to become so rich?"

"I'm pretty sure he was a railroad baron and owned a bunch of railroads in the 1800's which made him one of the wealthiest men at the time," Clark mused.

"Yes – that's correct. It says here he worked at an iron furnace in Greenwood New York for the Parrot family?"

"Yeah, they were a mining company owned by a family. They had iron mines all through that area." added Clark.

"So, apparently Edward Harriman got in the business of buying old bankrupt railroads, building them up and selling them which made him extremely successful and wealthy. Then when he died his wife got the whole estate – money and more than 20,000 acres of neighboring forest. It says here that she gifted the land to the state of New York in 1910 because she didn't want a prison built at Bear Mountain." Melody seemed fascinated by what she was reading.

"Yeah, Bear Mountain is where that nice lodge is, it's near West Point Military Academy. So that's how we got our park huh? Old Mrs. Harriman didn't want a prison…."

"Well, it looks like their children made out fairly well also…" continued Melody. "They had six children, it seems like the women married up and were socialites, and the sons…"

"Wasn't one son the governor of New York?" asked Clark.

"Yup dad – you're right. <u>William Averell Harriman</u> (1891-1986), wow he had a big career – he was the <u>Secretary of Commerce</u> under <u>President</u> <u>Harry S. Truman</u>, the <u>48th</u> <u>Governor of New York</u>, the U.S. Ambassador to the <u>Soviet Union</u>! and he was U.S. Ambassador to <u>Britain</u>. Seems he was married three times: First to Kitty Lanier Lawrance (from 1915 until their divorce in 1929), then <u>Marie Norton Whitney</u> (from 1930 until her death in 1970), then lastly <u>Pamela Beryl Digby Churchill Hayward</u> (from 1971 until his death in 1986). Apparently, Pamela became ambassador to France after helping Bill Clinton win the presidency. Wow – some families are really powerful huh? This is living proof of what wealth and a pedigree can do in this country," said Melody in disbelief.

"Yeah, but that's pretty normal – money and power tend to mix. Can you look up mining in Harriman and see if there is any history of the mining activities?" asked Clark.

"Sure –" Melody started searching words connected to mining and read what she was finding.

"It says here that the Parrot family used to mine iron in the area and operated several iron mines taking the ore to the Greenwood furnace during the civil war. There are other mines also, some from the 1700's….there was one that was a silver mine…." Melody slowed down as she flipped through the references.

"Go back to the iron mines – those would be the biggest right?" asked Clark.

"Dad, I don't know – what the hell do I know about mining?" Melody laughed.

"I know – neither do I! That's why we have to look this stuff up." Clark laughed.

"Ok – it says here the biggest of the iron mines in the Park is Bradley Mine."

"That's it! That's the one!" Clark exclaimed. "Read me more about Bradley Mine!"

"Ok dad, calm down," Melody was still smiling as she talked. " OK Bradley Mine, there are at least four or five blogs here from hikers and few pictures…wow its big…it says it's the biggest of the mines..and it's flooded… and it's in a section of the park that is restricted so no one should go hiking to it."

"That seems odd," reflected Clark. "That park has over 200 miles of trails through it including the Appalachian trail… there really is no section that's off limits…keep reading."

"Well maybe they don't want people hiking up to it and getting hurt. Maybe there is a fence around it."

"Do any of those trail blogs have directions?" Clark asked his daughter.

"Yes – they all do – they have precise directions and pictures. Dad, why are you so interested in this exact spot?"

Clark thought a minute and figured he could tell his daughter the truth about their excursion.

"Well Mel, it's like this…" Clark drew a deep sigh. "In 1973 there was a murder – a schoolteacher killed a seven year old who was selling magazine subscriptions – and he hid his body up at that mine."

Melody gasped "Oh my God! That's terrible! So why would you want to see it all these years later?"

"Well, way back when I was a rookie, I interviewed the murderer and he screamed at me about the mine and told me all the answers I needed were up there in the mine. I had done a huge amount of reporting on the case, but I had never gone to the site where the body was discovered," explained Clark.

"OK….but why go now…it's almost 50 years later," asked Melody, genuinely baffled.

Clark sighed. "Well, that scum bag is coming up for parole again and my ass clown editor Sean Caldwell assigned me a story where I interview him again and if I go down and see him.."

"You're going to make sure you do what HE asks? Dad come on…that makes no sense….he is a deranged killer….he is spouting nonsense. I'm loving our father daughter's ride and hike, but please tell me you aren't doing this to please the ravings of a madman who killed a child!" Melody tone was kind but sarcastic.

"Well Mel it's complicated.." Clark paused for a moment. "Back when I was a new reporter, that interview gave me a big break. But it wasn't as big a deal as the paper made it out to be, and if that happens a second time, I'm going to need all the background and material I can find…"

"To fake another story?" Melody laughed. "So, you're worried you are going to have to fudge it again and therefore you are taking directions from a child murderer."

"NO! I'm covering all bases. Plus – I always felt there was more to the case than what was in the papers and what my dad told me." Clark muttered.

"Your dad? You mean grandpa? What did he have to do with this?" asked Clark's daughter, bewildered.

"Oh…yeah…ummm…your grandfather was his defense attorney," Clark said quietly. "And he went with the defendant and the police to the spot where he hid the body."

"The next time you are worried whether I've had enough exercise….just let it go," giggled Melody. "And the next time you want to go on a father daughter hike, don't tell me anything….I don't need to know." Melody was jovial but somewhat uncomfortable by the details her father had shared.

They turned north onto Rt. 17 and over the state border into New York State. There was the town of Sloatsburg and Tuxedo and finally a right turn put them on Seven Lakes Drive and into the park. Suddenly there were no more houses. Continuous forest lined both sides of the road and a sign read "Lake Sebago". On their left a small lake lay still in peaceful solitude and on one area of shoreline were several cabins and a large dining hall like structure. It was one of the more than 40 camps built on more than 32 lakes in the park by the Civilian Conservation Corps in the 1930's. The CCC was a government funded project that tried to provide work to unemployed men during the great depression by sending them to build trials, camps, scenic rest areas and other utilities in state and national parks. Harriman Park was an ideal location for workers from New York City to arrive in a quick train ride to work in the summer months. The camps were also a perfect place for New York City school children to spend their summers away from the heat of the concrete jungle. Over the years, about half of the lakeside camps had been abandoned and fallen into disrepair. But half still functioned, some rented privately by church youth groups or other civic organizations. They drove past a ranger station with marked patrol vehicles in the driveway and a tall HAM radio antennae. Soon they drove to a circle with a sign that said Bear Mountain 9 Miles, Lake Welch 4 Miles, Lake Tiorati 2 Miles.

"Dad, it says go towards Lake Tiorati – turn here," said Melody.

They drove past two more lakes and came to another circle. There was a ranger booth in the middle and a very large parking area. A beach area on the lake had lifeguard chairs and a roped off area for swimming. Because it was so hot it was pretty empty.

"Ok it says turn at the Tiorati Circle and go towards the Elk Pen Parking area.." Melody read aloud. The car ascended a steep incline and Clark could feel the altitude pressure in his ears. "OK it says it's at the bottom of the hill here after the curve. Wait…slow down.." Melody was now intent on finding the exact spot. "Ok slower…in this photo it says there is a second white sign where the trail starts…and THERE!" Melody pointed to a plastic triangular sign nailed to a tree at eye level, barely visible from the road and obscured by the summer leaves.

"You sure this is it?" asked Clark as he looked for a place to pull off the road. He found a small gravel patch just barely big enough to fit his car.

"Yeah, this is it…at least it looks just like the photos. Look – that must be the trail," Melody pointed to a faint but distinct dirt path that weaved along the underbrush. It was the kind of trail that wasn't used every day but had been constructed deliberately and carefully.

"OK…let's try it – it looks pretty steep…" Clark realized that his invitation for Melody to get some exercise meant he was going to have to climb right alongside her. Before he could ask her if she thought they could make the steep ascent, she was already ahead of him scrambling up the gravelly surface in her running shoes.

"Come old man! You dragged me up here!" She shouted as Clark started to follow. The trail went at an almost 50-degree pitch and was made of loose dirt that slid under his shoes. He wasn't dressed for hiking, and he realized he should have done some basic preparation like wearing the right shoes. The trail wound upward around a huge boulder and then leveled off. Melody was waiting for him at the top of the steep section with a strange look on her face.

"Dad – feel that?" she asked as a cold wind blew over them in the July heat. The breeze was at least 10 to 15 degrees colder than the hot humid air and it seemed absolutely surreal to have a perfectly cold blast of air in the middle of the woods in July.

"That must be air coming from the mine. We must be close," said Clark out loud. He looked to his right and saw a deep crevasse in the rocks, one that was at least 20 feet high on either side. There were machinery marks in the walls of the adjoining precepes and Clark figured this must be the beginning of where the old equipment had cut and blasted its way through the bedrock. He and Melody entered the slotted rock columns around them and stepped carefully over sharp shards of shale and slate tailings that had been dumped when the mine was excavated. As they continued to walk, they reached a small bump of about six feet, and as they scrambled up the obstacle, their eyes were met with a cavernous opening 30 feet high. Another blast of even colder air hit their faces. Before them was a massive expanse that looked like a giant rock garage. Holes in the ceiling let streams of sunlight beam through giving the appearance of skylights. The floor of the giant room-like rock structure was muddy water. The mine had obviously flooded and though it branched into what looked like two tunnels, the water met the back wall in the darkness, with no opening or place to walk.

"Wow – this is really cool dad…!" said Melody. "But it's flooded so this is about as far as we can go huh? Where did he hide the body?"

"I don't know," Clark squinted to see the back wall some 40 feet away that was especially dark in the sunlight. He took a step forward as he was taking in the scenery and his foot caught something. He looked down to see a metal disc, seemingly attached to something underground. He bent down to get a closer look and rubbed his stubbed toe and saw a brass plate, in the shape of a circle.

"What was that – what did you just trip on?" asked Melody.

"I don't know…some metal fixture…doesn't look as old as everything else…" Clark bent down and looked closer, there was writing on the metal disc. It said, "Civil Defense Bunker 26 and COG HARRIMAN."

"What do you think that is dad?" asked Melody. Clark shook his head.

"I have no idea…but help me dig this out…I want to take it.."

Chapter 4

Clark sat at the conference table in the newsroom at the offices of the Newark Ledger turning over the medallion he had found at the entrance to the mine in his hand. It was a yellow circle with a blue triangle in the middle. It was made of metal, likely brass. He had a good sense of what the words "Civil Defense Bunker Harriman 26" meant. But elsewhere engraved on the edge of the circle in tiny letters the COG part of the identification eluded him. He pondered the strange object and turned it over in his hands oblivious to the conversations churning around him.

His editor, the insufferable Sean Caldwell, had insisted that every reporter that worked for the paper, regardless of whether they worked in news, features, sports or entertainment had to attend morning staff meetings. Even the obituary and classified section staff had to be there. The social media team was in the room also. Theoretically they were supposed to hear what the upcoming coverage and story assignments were in order to plan various social media initiatives which they would execute in tandem with whatever reporter had the assignment. But each editorial meeting became an opportunity for the much younger staffer to grandstand how wonderful their analytics were and how much traffic they had driven, combined with a "feedback report" summarizing what people were commenting and sharing about the newspaper's coverage. Clark had started working in a time when the morning editorial meeting was the only moment that the staff saw one another and communicated all day – a vital, necessary, organized effort at teamwork and coordination. These staff meetings were born out of necessity in an age before computers and cell phones. But those days were long gone, and Caldwell's predecessor, Steve Miller, had done away with morning editorial meetings fifteen years ago, instead relying on practical tools like group emails, texts, video conferencing and various technological advancements that made everyone's lives easier.

But as he oscillated between nostalgia and inferiority, presently Caldwell insisted that every morning the staff would file in like cattle, only to sit around an enormous conference table, announce what they were working on to face direct questioning and criticism from the editor in full view of everyone else. This was his way of marking his territory and the abject showmanship of an insecure boss. Steve Miller never had to do that because he was a real editor. Clark wasn't the only old dog in the room – there were still a few colleagues that had been around as long as he had – journalist crusaders with black ink in their veins who collectively had established the official historical record of the planet over the last decades. Morning after morning these masters of the written word would reveal upcoming stories in their respective sections born out of true wisdom and decades of reporter discretion, only to be told by an insolent 25-year-old it wouldn't "trend" or didn't have the potential to "go viral". Caldwell would often defer to these self-righteous youths who saw the world in adolescent overtime and change a story assignment, adjust its focus or cancel it altogether. It nauseated Clark not just because it was pathetic and transparent, but because each morning he watched real news die at that conference table. He watched colleagues he respected get belittled and shot down for doing their jobs well. Like an army left stranded long after a war had ended, journalism had lost its focus and mission to a shiny new distraction, and no one seemed to notice or care.

Elizabeth sat next to Clark fidgeting. He could tell she had something on her mind but his attitude that morning was one dejected indifference. She tore a sheet of paper in half and handed him a note that read: "We gotta talk later. And heads up Caldwell is about to call on you and sandbag whatever your new column idea is!" Part of him wondered what it was Elizabeth needed to speak to him about, another part didn't care. And as for the editor opposing any new column idea, Clark didn't even have one for him to reject that morning. He kept turning the medallion over in his hands, unable to escape the burning suspicion that it had something to do with what MacDougal had shouted at him about the answers being in the mine. Whatever was going to come next with this story was going to have to be after Clark determined the origin and meaning of the medallion marker, he had found in Harriman State Park.

Clark turned Elizabeth's note over to the blank side and scrawled in large letters: "Fuck Caldwell," smiled and handed it back to Elizabeth. She glared at him and shook her head.

"Westfield! Where are we with the MacDougal interview? The parole hearing is coming up and I haven't seen anything yet," barked the editor from the head of the table.

"Well, I've been doing some research," said Clark in a lethargic and indignant tone. "Also, I've put in the request to the Trenton state prison for the sit-down interview and as of this moment I don't have clearance or an interview date." Clark sounded satisfied with his response. In the silence that followed he realized all sets of eyes in the room were on him.

"I see..," replied Caldwell in a slow smug tone. "Tell me about your 'research' Westfield." The editor made air quotes when he said the word research. It was clear he was being facetious and antagonizing Clark in front of the staff.

"I'm happy to update you on my research when I have some material conclusions, Mr. Caldwell," Clark shot back in an equally bitter and antagonistic tone. He was not going to be belittled by the editor and as he glanced around the room, he saw several staff smile as they realized he was pushing back. Clark wasn't the only one who disliked Caldwell. Other than a few junior sycophants, the general feeling was that he was insecure, inept, and not to be trusted.

"If you had been paying attention you would have heard all the other departments give substantive updates, Clark." Said Caldwell in a slow voice trying to be cruel. "So now that we are all here and we all have time on this Monday morning, why not enlighten us on what your research has revealed." The two men stared at one another with the deep hatred and contempt that can only blossom when an employee and a supervisor are totally void of any respect for the other.

"Ok, since you feel it's appropriate for the sports team, the photography department, the classifieds, the obituary desk and the political teams to waste valuable reporting time hearing about the minutiae of my next piece, who am I to contradict you?" Clark smiled at Caldwell and then at the rest of the conference room where several staffers smiled back, and others shook their heads. They all knew Caldwell was a fool to take on Clark Westfield and he was certain to lose the big grandstand play. The staff waited in anticipation the way a classroom watches the cut-up student challenge a teacher with no fear of repercussions. Most smiled, however Elizabeth, seated next to Clark, simply stared at her laptop computer resting on her knees and made no eye contact with anyone.

"The last time I interviewed MacDougal, more than 25 years ago, he emphasized that there could be some exculpatory evidence at the site where he hid his victim," explained Clark to the rest of the room, ignoring the editor at the front of the table who had originated the question. There were a few older staffers in the room that had worked at the paper when Clark had conducted his first interview. They met his gaze and nodded. "So, I went through the original case files and reviewed the location. I then went in the field and examined the site making various observations regarding what the logistics of the crime entailed and the setting in which the evidence was collected." Clark purposely embellished the technical aspects of his excursion with Melody and as he filled his sarcastic response with hyper-jargon. The older staffers smiled completely aware of his tactic to ridicule Caldwell.

"You found the exact location?" challenged Caldwell. "What was the exact spot?"

"The exact spot was an abandoned iron mine in Harriman State Park over the border in New York State. Bradley mine to be exact. And yes, I found the exact spot." Clark replied smugly.

"And what did your visit to the mine reveal?" Caldwell asked. His tone had changed and once he realized that Clark had done some work on the case it was apparent, he had lost the supervision battle he chose to fight in front of the staff.

"I found this…" Clark let the brass medallion land on the conference table with a thud. The staff looked at it in silence. Sean Caldwell stared expressionless and unimpressed. After several seconds of silence, a voice spoke in the back of the room.

"That's a civil defense authority marker…let me see that." The voice belonged to Richie Byrne, a longtime political reporter and editor of the national desk. Richie Byrne was one of the few people who had been at the paper longer than Clark. He had started his career covering local and state politics in New Jersey in the late 1970's, graduated up to the Washington desk and now oversaw the section that reported on elections, local state and federal government news and all commentary and opinion pieces connected to politics. He had seen vast and drastic change in his tenure as an old Cold War sentinel. He was a stout man with a determined posture, unbothered by the trivial details of the day to day. In the late 60's, while his classmates were answering the draft and being shipped off to Vietnam to fight in the steaming jungles, Richie Byrne enlisted in the Navy as an engineer for submarine duty. He had earned his dolphin patch and disappeared under the waves for ten years. During his time in the Navy, he serviced Polaris missiles, which at the time were the tip of the spear on American attack subs. Those missiles, first deployed in the 1950's, were fired under the ocean at depths too far to detect, breaking the surface with a roar and zipping deep into the Soviet Union to release multiple warheads. Of course, he had only fired unarmed versions in training at friendly countries and Arctic wastelands, but that decade spent underwater had changed him. Like most of the men and women of the armed forces Clark had met over the years, Richie Byrne had a faraway stare in his eyes. He could be jovial, even delightful. But there was an awareness deep in his psyche that had seen what mankind was capable of and what would happen if a war with the Soviets ever started. Upon leaving the Navy full time, like so many former men and women of the service, Richie Byrne felt the best way to avoid almost certain dystopia was to ensure that public policy, along with the national mindset, was as smart and educated as possible and understood the stakes. He took work as a military consultant to papers like the Examiner that had a Washington bureau and served states like New Jersey that harbored McGuire Air Force base and the Naval Weapons Station at Earle. These military installations lay quietly and inconspicuously among a population of eight million New Jersey residents, and in the days before Wikipedia men like him were the only resource reporters like Clark could call when they were working a story. He saw his consultancy to reporters and media outlets as a continuation of his work on safeguarding and protecting the nuclear arsenal. Richie saw the vocation of journalism - or as he jokingly called it "civilian debriefing and engagement" - as man's only hope of avoiding the mutually assured destruction that served as the sole boundaries in the Cold War's three-dimensional chess. When the U.S.S.R. evaporated with a whimper in 1991, Richie Byrne and so many others like him became soldiers without a mission – wandering aimlessly until the day when a letter came from the Secretary of the Navy thanking them for their service informing them their orders ``would not be renewed.'' Unable to grasp the sudden disappearance of the threat of nuclear annihilation, those lonely and bleak days found Byrne solace at the bottom of a bottle of gin. After several months, Steve Miller showed up at his house needing his help for the reporting about the closure of Fort Dix. Seeing his plight, Miller hired him full time at the paper and had him cover town council meetings and later state politics in between any military coverage. It was there that Richie Byrne met a rookie Clark Westfield, whom he saw as a young bastard that somehow scored an interview with New Jersey's most hated child murderer. Their mutual contempt for the status quo and keen insight into man's darker impulses made them brothers in a shared mission. Over the years a long and deep friendship had developed between the two men. Nowadays, they talked less, socialized less, and did little more than acknowledge one another in the men's room and commissary. But the respect had never dissipated even a little. Whatever words they had for one another at this point in their career, though fewer, were meaningful. Perhaps even more meaningful than they had ever been…

"Ok…so you found a piece of metal garbage…," Caldwell said, expecting a laugh from the packed room that never came. "When is your interview with MacDougal in prison?"

Clark shook his head in obvious disgust in front of the staff.

"I'm waiting on the communications officer in the warden's office to give me the OK. These things take time Sean," said Clark in a tone that attempted to point out the editor's lack of field experience.

"Oh no worries…." Replied Caldwell with something odd about his smile. "I have a note from the warden right here, it says MacDougal has agreed to see you on a standard visiting day and the bureau of corrections has granted you permission for the interview. Standard visiting days are…oh..Tuesday….that's tomorrow..well that works out well doesn't it? I'll expect a draft on Wednesday. Please record the interview. Great work Westfield!" Caldwell smiled and stacked the papers in front of him and got up to adjourn the meeting. Some of the staff around the room chuckled that he had arranged the interview behind Clark's back. Clark sat in silence glaring at his editor as he walked out the conference room door and was followed by the multitude of workers. He had been upstaged and outplayed in an overtly hostile move.

"I know what you are thinking, Westfield," a voice said as Richie Byrne sat down next to him. "He's not worth it, you'll have your chance. We need to find a place to talk where the walls don't have ears.." Clark nodded and the two men walked out of the conference room, into the elevator and down to the ragingly hot Newark streets.

"The usual place?" Clark asked as Richie Byrne stared intently straight ahead. Byrne nodded and said nothing.

A half hour later Clark let his eyes adjust to the dimly lit foyer of a place called the Little Theater. A fixture on Broad Street in Newark since the early 1960's, the Little Theater had a decrepit and fading neon sign that buzzed and flickered vomit colored pink and green luminescence. It had shown pornographic movies in an age long before VCRs made it an option in the privacy of every household. A throwback to the golden age when the porn theater industry that was run by the mafia, the Little Theater somehow survived the home video cassette revolution that shuttered adult theaters and improved neighborhoods all across the country by switching over to gay movies. In an age before apps on a cell phone let people of all fetishes meet one another anonymously, places like the Little Theater were a crossroads of perversion, confusion, drugs and sociopaths. Clark had done an investigative series on the theater and its unusual survival in the late 1990's. During his reporting, he had spotted and been spotted by Richie Byrne in the back of the theater. Afterwards, Clark took him aside back in the newsroom to let him know that his secret and personal habits were of no interest to him or the story. It was during one of these conversations that Richie let him know he was there to meet a source, and that the theater was owned by a political operative that regularly fed him information about elected officials. If one rose to a certain level in politics in New Jersey you had to deal with various unsavory factions that were stakeholders in election outcomes, and there was no better way to compromise a politician than to gather material for blackmail collected at a gay porn theater. Richie had even taken Clark along a few times when they had seen mayors, state senators, even a congressman appear at the theater, participate in the various extracurricular activities that went on and leave, never knowing they had been photographed or recorded. When Richie Byrne needed information at a later time or needed someone to apply pressure for an interview, he could leverage everything that had been collected. There were many afternoons that Clark showed up at the newsroom and an envelope would be waiting on his desk containing photographs that had been given to Richie, compromising a politician which Clark could then decide to use at the right time when he needed someone to talk to. Their racket had worked for decades. Clark and Richie both slept with a clear conscience, figuring the various politicos and power brokers they were pressuring were already up to no good and it was incumbent on the two reporters to use all tools at their disposal in their crusade against corruption. Clark figured no one else played by the rules so why should he when covering them? The two men had no opinion on the seedy nature of the place, in fact over the years they had grown desensitized and bored with the atmosphere, and the rest of the world had tired of the salacious underpinnings as well. Nothing that went on in the Little Theater was news any longer - in fact it wasn't even interesting to even the most sheltered person.

"There was a time that when you told me to meet here it was because a governor's chief of staff was buying meth in the back," Clark laughed and sat down next to Richie in the last row of the theater. "God we were great weren't we Rich? Remember all the stories we broke out of this dump? Such a piece of fetid nostalgia..."

"It's good to see you, Westfield," Richie Byrne fist bumped Clark and looked around to see if anyone was in earshot. "Yeah, there was a time when people gave a shit about who showed up in a place like this. Of course, nothing is shocking anymore and trying to lean on a source because you saw them in a gay porn theater is about as effective as saying you saw someone run a red light." Richie shook his head and smiled.

"You sure you don't just come here for the ambiance?" asked Clark, ribbing him a little bit.

"Honestly, I do come here for comradery – but it's not what you think. I got to know the guys that work here at my AA meetings over the years. Despite how disgusting this place is, they are all decent guys, all fighting to stay sober another day and they are the most real people you'll ever meet..." said Richie Byrne with a shrug.

"Whatever floats your boat Byrne…You know I don't judge.." said Clark laughing and shaking his head. "Seriously though, if I have to sit in front of a screen watching two dudes pound each other this must be serious…what is it you need to tell me?"

"Two things," Richie's demeanor got deadly serious. "First – word back at the office is that Caldwell is gunning for you. He has been talking it up to the new owners and he is setting traps for you, hoping you'll hang yourself and he is ready to pounce. He has laid out a restructuring plan for the coming year and some people are gonna get clipped. He's got you on the execution list."

"Yeah, I figured," sighed Clark. "He can't touch me, I'm in the union. He can't fire me without cause. Plus, I'm not afraid of that prick Caldwell. The guy couldn't find his own ass if his life depended on it, and he wouldn't know news if it bit him in the ass. Thanks for the heads up, but it's not like it's a mystery we hate each other."

"I'm looking out for you brother, and this is different. He has already turned in his action steps memo and if they sign off on it, there won't be a thing the union can do to protect you," said Richie with genuine concern.

"Well maybe I've been at it too long, Rich," sighed Clark. "The job isn't what it used to be – you know that better than anybody. Even if we turn a big story, the general public out there doesn't seem as bothered by corruption and bad behavior. It's like society just gave up on right and wrong because it was too much work. Now they just exist in their social media bubbles and their self-fellating feedback loops, and don't get me started on the younger generation and how clueless they are…"

"Yeah, I know, there is no longer room for old dogs like us," Richie interrupted Clark. "And I know you know you've got a target on your back with Caldwell, and you'll survive. I've always got your back but there is only so much I can do. But that's not the main reason we needed to talk." Richie leaned in and spoke in an even lower voice glancing around to see if anyone was within earshot. "Let me see that medallion you found – you have it with you?" Clark nodded and handed him the brass disc. "Wow…that's the real thing alright.." Richie stared at the object and turned it over in his hands.

"You brought me to a safe house in a gay porn theater to take a closer look at this medallion I found in the woods? We could have done this back in the office….anything you need to tell me Richie?" Clark teased his friend though he could sense there was something serious he was about to hear.

"You don't know what this is do you?" asked Richie Byrne. holding it and waving it in a display.

"I just figured it's a marker of some kind…maybe for surveying?" replied Clark.

"Clark, this is a Civil Defense Marker," said Richie in a low voice. "These were placed at the entrances to bunkers that had been built all over the country in the 1950's and 60's. There were places set up in the event of a nuclear war that had food, supplies, medical equipment and communications that were safe from radiation and where people could live and hide during an attack."

"OK – so you mean a bomb shelter like the ones that were in post offices and libraries? So, what – those were everywhere back then," asked Clark perplexed.

"Yeah, but what makes this one different is the letter COG." explained Riche. That stands for Continuity of Government. Certain secure bunkers were created for leadership to be safely housed so

Congress, the military and the president could keep running things if a war ever broke out. They also had detailed plans and manuals that contained laws and protocols to rebuild society if everyone got wiped out. A COG site wasn't just a run of the mill fallout shelter where people like you and I could go – it was an elite secret location that was for the most important government officials and essential personnel. They were in various places around the country, but only the Pentagon knew all the locations and they were highly classified. You somehow found a marker that came from one of these sites – you may have stumbled on one."

Clark looked at Richie in the darkness and the seriousness of his expression made him realize the significance of the medallion.

"OK…well why was it up in the middle of the woods?" Clark wondered aloud.

"Well, it wasn't there by accident Westfield – that's what I'm trying to tell you. And it's not a fake either. Nobody knows how to make a counterfeit marker like this – and see where it says Harriman 26 here?" Richie ran his finger along the raised letter around the edge of the brass disc. "That means there was a bunker nearby and that was its designation. You may have thought you were up in the middle of the woods, but you were probably really close to the entrance and didn't realize it."

"We were standing at the entrance to an old flooded iron mine….there was nothing up there…" Richie cut him off mid-sentence.

"That's it…! It's probably not a mine at all. That must be the entrance to a Civil Defense Bunker that was an elite COG site! Westfield you gotta take me there – I gotta see this place!" Richie Byrne's voice was growing louder in the darkness of the seedy theater.

"Ok but it was flooded – you can't get in. It's a big, cavernous entrance but it only goes back about 80 feet and there are two pools of water and that's really all there is…" Clark was nowhere near as excited as his colleague and his mind was wandering to how he was going to outmaneuver his editor and not lose his job.

"Ok – listen – you gotta go do that prison interview that Caldwell told you to.."

"You mean the one he hijacked on me? That fucking prick thinks he is such hot shit communicating with the prison warden…30 year ago I would have punched him right at the conference table."

"Wait…Clark…you are interviewing that murderer MacDougal, right?" asked Richie

"Yeah – and I'm not looking forward to it…why?" answered Clark.

"Why did you go to the mine for research?" asked Richie intently.

"Well, that's where he hid his victim back in 1973. I interviewed him 25 years ago and he screamed at me that there were answers up there in the mine, so I figured after all this time I'd go take a look at where he hid the boy's body and at least I'd have seen it for myself…."

"So he told you to go there….." muttered Richie softly.

"Yeah… why? The guy is a psycho…he killed a 7-year-old. He says all kinds of crazy shit…."

"Clark…find out why he was telling you to go there," said Richie with a dead serious expression. "That's important…there is a reason he went to that location."

Clark sighed. The thought of any dialog with MacDougal on any topic triggered surges of anxiety deep in Clark's inner child.

"Ok I'll see what I can shake out of him. The guy is a lunatic. I think you are reading way too much into this Rich," Clark said. "Plus, I love that you know your cold war history, but this medallion could have been a prop from a fraternity playing a game of paintball or something. Now we can get out of here please? I know you love the ambiance of the loud gay sex on the screen but it's starting to creep me out…"

"That's no prop…" said Richie Byrne looking Clark dead in the eyes and not reacting to his joke. And just like that the two men left.

As Clark rolled down his driver's side car window to hand over his identification at the guard booth the July heat hit him like a steam blast. The Trenton State prison was an aberration of architecture – faded painted bricks sizzled behind a 20-foot hurricane fence topped with coils of razor wire. The ugly nondescript building was a physical testament that any time spent behind its walls was a form of punishment for anyone that entered – including employees, visiting family members and even reporters who had to secure an interview. Inside that wretched façade were more than two thousand prisoners, many of them worse human beings than Joseph MacDougal. Clark couldn't help feeling that when he drove through that gate, he crossed an invisible line behind which a human conscience was optional – and several of the residents and many of the guards hadn't taken the option.

The corrections officer who took his identification entered his name in the computer in the booth, then picked up the phone to call the reception area. He then handed back Clark his ID and said in a hoarse voice:

"Ok Mr. Westfield, proceed up to the entrance you'll see the visitor parking on your right. Your colleague is here and waiting for you inside."

"Colleague? What colleague? I'm not working with anyone here today." Clark said, perplexed.

"I don't know sir, I just started my shift, it just says here there are two passes that were reserved for you today and you are the second to arrive," replied the guard with complete disinterest. Clark thought a minute and assumed there must have been a mistake. After all, one doesn't wind up a prison parking attendant after getting perfect SATs. Then a thought struck Clark….he realized that Sean Caldwell had communicated with the prison without his knowledge and while unlikely, there was a very good chance he may have shown up for the interview. If that were the case, there was no better place for a man-to-man dick measuring contest than a prison parking lot and that would have pushed Clark over the line. He felt distant rage slowly start to simmer in his guts, and it was a welcome distraction from the reality that he would soon be sitting down with a face that had haunted him since he was 8 years old. The buzzer on the doors unlocked the large steel latch and Clark pushed through to the waiting area. There was no air conditioning, and the inside was as hot as an oven. As he turned to the plexiglass window there seated in the waiting area was Elizabeth Cranford. As her eyes met his, she stood up at attention and walked over to Clark with an anxious expression on her face. So, the guard at the parking lot booth was correct – but what was she doing here? She stood in front of Clark for several seconds, the silence between them was as heavy as the humid July air.

"Clark…let me explain…" she stammered.

"Did Caldwell send you?" Clark asked. Elizabeth nodded.

"Look, I've been trying to get some time with you.. he told me I had to come to the interview with you. I don't want this story, I don't want to be here, I don't want to be anywhere near this - you can go in there without me and when you're done we gotta talk."

"But you still came Liz..didn't you?" said Clark smartly.

"He's gunning for you Clark and he is putting me in the middle of it. Cut me some slack here. – I'm trying to help. Go do your interview and afterwards we can figure out what to do.." Elizabeth was clearly troubled by the situation, and it was evident she didn't appreciate being manipulated by her editor.

"Nah, Liz, come in with me. It will be good for you. Every good reporter needs to do at least one interview with a maniacal killer. I don't know if he will talk to you or not, but if he doesn't then we can just tell Caldwell he blew the whole thing by sending you." Clark rolled his eyes.

A corrections officer beckoned them through a set of double doors and down a dank corridor. The whole building smelled of dampness, urine, infection and failed humanity. The prison was a physical manifestation of mankind's worst instincts. Male prisoners in jumpsuits passed them in the hallway, some pushing meals or laundry carts. One carried a mail bag. All of them stopped and looked Elizabeth up and down, making no attempt to hide their stares.

"I bet you are a real treat for these guys to see," sniped Clark as Elizabeth tried not to pay attention. The guard led them to a room and indicated they should have a seat at a conference table where two chairs were arranged opposite a third. The door shut and they sat in the room in silence under gray, fluorescent lights that made the world look moldy and sterile.

"I'm gonna let you do the talking," said Elizabeth, clearly nervous. Clark glared at her before breaking into a smile. She smiled back nervously.

After a few minutes, footsteps could be heard in the hallway and the door swung open. A guard walked in followed by Joseph MacDougal and two additional corrections officers. The first guard spoke:

"Mr. Westfield, we will be outside. Any issues just give a tap on the door. You are cleared for no more than 30 minutes," Clark nodded in acknowledgement. Joseph MacDougal slowly walked to the chair opposite Clark and Elizabeth and sat down. He stared intently at Clark and rested his elbows on the table to show his writs were shackled. A chain was clipped to the middle of the wrist restraints and joined a second set of shackles around his ankles on a frame length chain. He was a tall man – perhaps six foot seven inches. His frame was stocky and muscular. His hands were enormous. He wore his hair in a crew cut and there were several days of facial hair around his chin. A scar ran from his left eye socket down under his jawbone.

"Nice to see you again Mr. Westfield. Even nicer that you brought a friend," said MacDougal still staring directly at Clark as he indicated Elizabeth.

"Yeah, uh, thanks for agreeing to talk with us Mr. MacDougal," stammered Clark. "As you know, there is a parole hearing coming up and.."

"I only agreed to talk with you. I didn't say you could bring a friend," said MacDougal, still not acknowledging Elizabeth. "Did you go and look where I told you to Mr. Westfield?" His tone was soft, even and bloodcurdling cold.

"Well actually yes. The last time we spoke you suggested I check out the mine where they found the victim. So, when I heard you were willing to talk to me again I took a ride up and looked around," replied Clark. He had already lost control of the interview and could feel his spine start to tingle.

"And what did you find?" he asked, still not breaking his intense stare.

"Well, not much," said Clark, hoping the murderer would reveal what it was he was supposed to be looking for. "It's a nice state park and all, quite a steep hike..but there was nothing of any real note…not that I found anyway."

"Then we've got nothing to discuss," hissed MacDougal and he started to rise from his seat. "Thanks for bringing your friend..been a while since I've seen such a pretty lady. She will give me plenty to think about later.." he said with a creepy grin.

"Wait, let's talk a bit Joe," pleaded Clark. "I went up and looked around but your hearing is coming up in two weeks and I think you should tell your side of the story.. I mean a lot of people want to know…"

"They all want to know why, right? They want to know why I killed that boy? YOU want to know why I killed him too, don't you? It's nagged at you since you were a little boy…" MacDougal was smiling a maniacal smile as he taunted Clark. "Well Mr. Westfield, I told you to go find out and it looks like you found nothing..so best of luck to you putting your story together." MacDougal tapped on the door to let the guards know he was ready to leave.

"Well wait a minute…" Clark turned and tried to think of some way to get MacDougal to stay and talk longer. "I did find this.." Clark took the medallion out of his pocket and placed it on the table with a clink.

Joseph MacDougal looked at the metal object and his whole demeanor changed.

"Oh Jesus…" he gasped as he instantly collapsed to the ground and began shaking violently. MacDougal's body convulsed and his feet hit the legs of the table and the chairs. The metal chains of his handcuffs scraped violently as his body wretched. Elizabeth stood up and got out of the way. Two guards ran into the room and attempted to get control of his massive tremors. He moaned inaudibly like a man struggling to breathe. Foam oozed from his lips and smeared across the floor. His head hit the leg of the table and a small gash trickled a drop of blood into the lines on his forehead. He was having a seizure. The guard shouted for Clark and Elizabeth to leave the room as two more ran down the hallway and helped the attending officers. After almost 90 seconds, Joseph MacDougal's convulsions stopped, and he lay motionless in a pool of his own spit, snot and blood. His prison jumpsuit was wet with urine. His lifeless body lay still on the floor.

"Get me the medical unit now!" barked one of the guards. An officer in the hallway spoke into his radio, paging medical assistance…

Clark and Elizabeth stood in the hallway stunned. The interview was over.

Chapter 5

Richie Byrne sat in his office at the newspaper. He hesitated a moment. He was planning to call an old source at the Pentagon and ask a few questions. His source, a former Lieutenant Colonel in the Army, had been an advisor to the Joint Chiefs of Staff and worked in Army Intelligence since the early 70's. The source had been a great go to whenever Richie Byrne was covering defense budget allocations. Byrne would usually repeat or show what the various congressmen and senators on the armed services committees were telling him about money spent on defense and where it went, and his source would verify whether it was true or not. In one case in the late 1980's, Byrne had identified a huge gap in the budget and wanted to report that it was being used for various black ops – operations so secret that they didn't exist on paper and only a handful of people ever knew they happened. His source had told him the Pentagon had asked for, been granted and put in to use millions of dollars for radiation detectors around Manhattan in response to rumors that the Soviet Union had installed suitcase sized nuclear weapons in apartments and office buildings. Of course, it had turned out to be a wild goose chase and no mini nuclear weapons were ever discovered – but the story break had put Richie

Byrne on the map and led to many other Pentagon staffers that wanted

to provide information they thought the public should know but were

prohibited from revealing. As the stories increased in frequency and

importance, Richie's relationship with his source had grown more and

more complicated. Not because it was a military intelligence officer

revealing classified information about national security to a newspaper

reporter, but because she was a woman and Richie was a man and over

time when men and women spend a lot of time together on

complicated matters, the big picture and wavelengths between them

can get equally complicated. They had had a sordid affair which had

ended in some pretty hurt feelings and not spoken to one another in

four years. Dialing her number took all the strength he had left as a

lonely middle-aged man in a loveless and sexless marriage – but

something told him there was something important about the story

Clark Westfield was working on. He needed answers and well….he

dialed…

"Hello, it's me…it's been a while," said Richie when he heard the click on the other end as Lieutenant Colonel Kelly Pram picked up the phone. Several seconds of silence followed.

"Richie…how have you been," asked a female deep baritone voice.

"Fine, er, good. Good to talk to you," stammered Richie. There was no hiding the awkwardness in the conversation. "So, I know it's been a few years since we've spoken, but I had a couple questions that came up on a story a colleague was working on, and you would normally be the person I would call on something like this and…well…I just figured,"

"You just figured you would call me up and walk back into my life like everything was fine?" prosecuted Lt. Col. Kelly Pram. "You know I waited a long time for this day when my phone was going to ring, and it would be you on the other end. I rehearsed my angry speech hundreds of times." She paused to chuckle briefly. "But somehow I'm not feeling that way.."

"Yeah well…let me start with an apology about everything. I've rehearsed what I was going to say a thousand times as well,"

Richie strained to keep his voice from breaking. "I guess I just want to let you know I feel really bad about everything, and I hope you are doing well."

"And you need help on a story?" shot back Lt. Colonel Pram.

"Well yeah, that too.."

"Yeah sure. Well, I'm NOT doing well and I've gotten divorced since we last spoke. I won't go into it. It's not your fault, but you didn't make anything easier. Let's just talk about why you called, shall we?" said Lt. Col. Pram with a military level firmness.

Several more moments of silence followed.

"Gee Kelly I'm really sorry about your divorce," gushed Richie. The conversation was starting to turn as cathartic as he anticipated.

"Until further notice, I'd prefer you call me Lieutenant Colonel Pram," she said in a stern voice. Richie, taken aback, managed to mutter a weak "Sure" in response. Then he heard Kelly Pram's voice break with laughter.

"You really are an easy mark," chuckled the Colonel. Richie smiled at his desk. He deserved some ribbing.

"Ok, well – moving on!" he said in a jovial tone. "You remember the series I wrote a few years back about the new Continuity of Government bunkers that were being built and you were the one that gave the info on the black sites and the black budgets that were designated outside the main defense budget?"

"Of course," coughed Lt Colonel Pram. "That little favor almost cost me my job and career. No thanks to you of course." He couldn't tell whether her tone was lighthearted or genuinely resentful.

"Well, I came across something interesting," continued Richie. "Were any of the new COG sites up in an area of New York State near the New Jersey border? Specifically, Harriman State Park?" Richie's voice was inquisitive.

"Harriman? No, of course not. None of the NEW sites would have been in Harriman, why?" asked Colonel Pram

"Wait…what do you mean of course not?" asked Richie. "Am I missing something?"

"Well, the Harriman bunkers are some of the first and oldest that were ever built – dating way back to the 1950's," explained colonel Pram. "In fact, it was Averell Harriman himself that came up with the general concept and showed it to President Eisenhower. He had spent his childhood exploring all the old mines up on the family property and suggested they would make great safety bunkers, and he further realized that there were abandoned mines all over the country that could be re-fitted and re-built as safety bunkers. Most were deep enough to avoid radiation fallout; most were well mapped and …"

"Wow! Did you say mines?!?" exclaimed Richie. "Tell me everything you know about the mines…!" he sounded as if he had been suddenly bitten by a snake.

Lt. Col. Pram laughed. "OK – take it easy. Many of the cold war protection bunkers were built in old mines provided the structures were stable because the locations were already known, and the depth made them environmentally sound for both radiation and blast. Harriman is only about 30 miles north of New York City, so it was a prime evacuation route and a perfect distance for any government, finance or foreign dignitaries in the event of Defcon 2. You can even get to it by boat as the Hudson River easily manages oil tanker traffic across along the lower park section. It's navigable as far north as Albany. "

"Finance? What do you mean finance?" asked Richie bewildered.

"Well, New York City houses both the New York Stock exchange and the NASDAQ as well as a large portion of the world's gold reserves," she continued. "Those aren't just average people working down in the financial nerve center of the globe and there is a special national security interest in preserving both staff and materials from both, so essential personnel had bunker assignments which would have been in proximity to the city and I'm sure some would have been the Harriman sites."

"When you say assignments, what exactly do you mean?" asked Richie.

"Well like I said," said the Colonel in a self-satisfied voice. "The government and the Pentagon had created various lists which still exist to this day of government, defense and private sector personnel who had instructions to report to a specific location – usually the secure bunker closest to them – if we reached Defcon 2. They knew to stop what they were doing and report to their assigned location."

"So, there were private citizens that were on lists as part of the Defcon contingency plans?" asked Richie.

"Of course! As you know from your time in the military, the Defcon scale are defense readiness measurements in response to world events," Colonel Pram's voice was rambling in a military style monotone. " Five is the constant and sought after status without conflict and as circumstances change, the Defcon scale counts down from 5 to 1 which indicates various levels of troop readiness and movements, etc. Defcon 2 is the last stage before actual nuclear war. It means the missiles are prepped and ready and that the Strategic Air Command is already flying or can be in the air in 15 minutes and as you know from your tour underneath the waves, the attack submarines are in position and locked on targets."

"Believe it or not, on both my tours there wasn't a lot of discussion about protocols for *after* we fired the missiles," Richie reflected.

"Yeah well, your commanders had them and if it were necessary, you would have been told," said Colonel Pram. "Also, the last thing you want is for troops to know where the after-party is in a war, so they aren't tempted to desert the battlefield and show up later or god forbid have the enemy torture it out of them if captured."

"Geez – you aren't making me miss my time in the military," Richie laughed. "Ok, so here is what I've got: A colleague of mine was looking around up at one of the mines in Harriman. He says it was flooded, but he found a brass marker and it's got the Civil Defense logo pressed into it – the circle with the triangle and its painted Blue and Yellow – but it's also got COG Harriman 26 stamped in it. That means it's a Continuity of Government site, right?"

"Yes, that is what the COG indicator means," said Kelly Pram. "And as you know, a COG site was much different than a routine civil defense bunker. It had substantial resources for longer stays, communications equipment, usually HAM radios, various military grade ciphers, medical equipment and manuals and most had a weapons allocation. It wouldn't surprise me that the Harriman COG site was one of the bigger ones. The legend is that Averell Harriman always got what he wanted. Ambassadors usually do. Why was your colleague up there?"

"Well, that's a random element," responded Richie. "My colleague, it's Clark Westfield by the way - you remember Clark? Anyway, he was researching a 40 plus year old murder case and the psycho that killed a seven-year-old boy and hid his body up there. So, when he went to go take a look at the crime scene he stumbled on the marker. But the mine is flooded so I guess if there was a bunker then it's all under water now."

"Actually, not necessarily!" exclaimed Colonel Pram. "First, all the civil defense bunkers had multiple entrances – so the water would have been only at the front entrance and only temporarily. The bigger COG bunkers usually had trigger explosives that would drain the water and were hydro engineered in a way that would instantly cause an away flow and reveal an entrance. Usually, the flood entrances were at the top of a hill. The alternative entrance would have a fuse box with a panic switch that the first arriving Department of Defense official would activate and bang! - the water at the front entrance would be gone. But wait – what about this murder? When did this happen?"

"Oh – that," Richie responded. "It's a terrible case. It happened in 1973. This boy selling magazine subscriptions for scouts knocked on this sick bastard's door. He let him in, raped him, killed him, and then hid his body up in the mine. Westfield has to do a story because the dirtbag is up for parole if you can believe it. He has been badgering Westfield about the mine for some reason so when Clark went up there, this was the only thing he saw and of course it's got nothing to do with the crime. I just thought it might make an interesting feature story about cold war nostalgia," Richie paused for several seconds. "And it was an excuse to say hello."

More seconds of silence followed. Richie wondered if he had caught her off guard with his attempted olive branch of amends.

"What was this guy's name?" asked Colonel Pram coldly.

"The perpetrator? Joseph MacDougal. He is serving 25 to life in Trenton State Prison. Why?" Richie asked, somewhat disappointed she didn't acknowledge his attempt to mend fences.

"OK…Rich…I gotta call you back." Lt. Col. Kelly Pram hung up the phone abruptly. Richie sat in stunned silence for several moments.

"Sometimes you just can't win," he muttered to himself.

Clark sat in his car in the parking lot of the paper's office building. The morning show coming through the radio crackled with static and other annoying audio effects that made him quickly flip the knob as the digital display screen went blank and the device shut off. To begin the day with a friendly voice, a companion unobtrusive, was something that Clark always relished and helped him get his aging sleep deprived frame to the job each day. But this morning, with its higher-than-normal sleep deficit, he was in no mood for cheeky upbeat jokes and listener contests. He kept envisioning the convulsing frame of a large man in a prison jumpsuit and the bloodshot whites of his eyes as they had rolled deep back in his head. As Clark had tried to interview Joseph MacDougal, the confessed murderer had suddenly undergone a seizure. This meant several things – first, that the brass medallion Clark showed him may have triggered it somehow – and second – he had no interview and no story to show his editor. Exactly what he was going to do about it was eluding him and keeping him seated in his car before going into work. He didn't know if he was going to get a second shot at another interview, and most likely he wouldn't. So, he sat, thinking. He needed something to mitigate the fact he was walking empty handed, again.

He dialed the number on his cell phone for Dr. Darria Long, an emergency room physician that he had met when his daughter was hospitalized after a school bus accident. They had become friendly and because the hospital was such a large advertising client of the newspaper, Clark had helped her get a basic first aid advice column and introduced her to the newsroom so the beat reporters could call her for stories. She answered when she saw his contact info flash the incoming call.

"Hi darling! Wow, it's early for you to be calling! Everything ok? Do you need my expert quoted opinion or did you smash your finger with a hammer?" joked Dr. Darria in her singsong voice. The heavy New Jersey humidity hung over the open windows of the car like a wet blanket. He could feel the slime of sweat between his shoulder blades adhering him to the seat.

"Hey Darria, sorry to call you so early," muttered Clark in a gravelly morning voice. "Something strange happened yesterday and I wanted to ask…"

"Wait! How is Melody? Did you tell her I was asking for her?" interrupted Dr. Darria in her perky tone.

"Melody is fine.." laughed Clark. "I'll tell her you said hello. But I need to ask you about seizures.."

"Oh, good lord she didn't have a seizure, did she?" gushed Darria in a worried blurt.

"No, it's not about Melody," replied Clark. "I was doing an interview yesterday and the guy I was interviewing suddenly had a seizure."

"Oh. Is he ok? Did you call an ambulance?" asked Dr. Darria.

"Yeah, he is fine – he was a prisoner so we were at the prison and the guards took care of it, but it was the most disturbing thing to see. He suddenly started shaking and thrashing and making horrible sounds. Stuff gushed out of his mouth and nose… it was really awful."

"Yeah, that sounds about right – seizures are very traumatic for people to see." explained Dr. Darria. "Was this the first time you'd ever witnessed one?"

"Yes, believe it or not!" answered Clark. "I'd actually never seen one before and had no idea how violent the convulsions were. He banged his head against the leg of the table at one point too – that's gonna hurt. But I don't really know a lot about them, I don't know what's normal and what's not – like I said this was a first for me. What causes them? What happens during them? What is recovery like? I'm gonna have to figure out how to go back and see this guy again so I need to know what I am dealing with."

"Sure – and let me know if I'm being quoted," joked Darria. "Think of a seizure as an electrical short circuit in the brain. You know when your computer crashes or your cell phone just freezes up? That's your brain when it has a seizure. You have millions of neurons firing all kinds of information through electrical impulses and the brain needs very specific and refined chemistry for all the different tasks it performs. When those signals get confused, crossed, compromised or disrupted, your brain can crash like a computer and wham!"

"And that's what caused the shaking and the moaning?" asked Clark.

"The shaking and moaning that you describe doesn't happen in every kind of seizure," explained Darria further. "There are many kinds of seizures that look nothing like that, sometimes you only know someone has seized if they are being neurologically monitored. The classic violent shaking is usually the kind of seizure produced by epilepsy – and in medicine we call these unprovoked."

"Unprovoked?" asked Clark. "You mean as opposed to seizures that can be provoked? How exactly would you provoke a seizure?"

"Well, a provoked seizure is one that has a cause other than epilepsy," continued Dr. Darria. "A whole range of medical conditions can provoke a seizure, such as dehydration, hypoglycemia, sometimes diabetes or alcohol withdrawal. But from what you are describing it sounds like your interview subject was a classic epileptic and he was experiencing symptoms."

"Ok that makes me feel better," sighed Clark. "The whole thing was so weird – everything was going fine, then I showed him this medallion and he immediately started convulsing – I was afraid somehow I might have caused it."

"Well, there are triggers for an epileptic seizure – many in fact. Someone living with epilepsy sometimes will be lucky enough to identify their unique individual triggers and can then avoid them throughout their life," said Darria as Clark's spirits sank. "That's why there is a warning PSA in theaters and concerts when a strobe light will be used. There are a whole range of electrical signals that might be triggers – it depends on the patient and the area of the brain responsible for the epilepsy. In addition to the treatment for a patient of identifying triggers and avoiding them, there are many drugs with a huge range of efficacies and side effects. However, I've never heard of a medallion being a visual trigger for epilepsy. That's a first – however, extreme stress can be a trigger so if your medallion stressed this guy out enough then BOOM! Maybe you did send him off to the races." Dr. Darria giggled.

"So maybe I did set this guy off…" mumbled Clark.

"Well don't be so hard on yourself there Clark," chimed Darria. "If you did it would have had to have been an extraordinary stressor for this man and it would have had to disrupt his brain activity enough to fire all the neurons in both hemispheres of the brain to total overload. How could that be possible?"

"You'd be surprised…" Clark's voice trailed off and he thanked her for her time and hung up the phone. He sat in his car digesting what he had just heard. A stressor so extraordinary that it would have to cause an overload of his neurons in both hemispheres of his brain to fire and crash his mental software. Could murdering a seven-year-old boy be extraordinary enough?

Clark's reflective moment was interrupted by a tap on the window. Elizabeth was outside in her running gear. Earbuds beaded with sweat protruded from her ears and the fluorescent yellow sports bra shirt was soaked with sweat in the July heat. Clark rolled down the window.

"You certainly make me feel overdressed," he said sarcastically.

"Listen you and I gotta talk. Can I get in?" painted Elizabeth as she opened the passenger door and sat down.

"By all means…make sure your sweat soaks into my car seat," Clark said as he rolled his eyes. "Look, I know yesterday was a bust and I'm sorry. I'm thinking that I'll call the warden again, check on MacDougal's condition, and see if we can go back again for an interview. I know the parole hearing is in a few days and Caldwell is going to flip out but fuck him. The guy had a goddam seizure and there is nothing we could have done about it." Clark looked far off into the distance with an expression of defeated disappointment.

"That's what I gotta talk to you about," Elizabeth was trembling with anxiety and Clark knew something was wrong. "Listen you were my first boss, my mentor, a friend…we've had our differences, but you are one of the most important people in my life…and…" Elizabeth's eyes filled with tears.

"Geez Liz – just say it," interrupted Clark. "We've known each other since you were a junior in college and I'm a big boy. What's on your mind?"

"The reason Caldwell sent me with you is because he plans on firing you and is saying he is going to make me city editor," she paused and sniffled. "I hate the whole idea. I hate him. I feel so duplicitous with you. He made me swear not to tell anyone, but I owe you the loyalty and I don't want to see you get fired." Elizabeth stopped talking and looked at Clark. He met her expression with a look of slight surprise and then the corners of his mouth gradually bent into a smile.

"Well congratulations!" boomed Clark with a huge grin. "You're going to be city editor! My little shaker Liz is growing up!"

"What do you mean? Aren't you angry with me?" asked Elizabeth.

"Angry?" Clark replied. "No, I'm not angry with you! You deserve it! You'll make an excellent city editor – and Newark needs you watching over it! Don't worry about me. You don't think I know that Caldwell has been trying to fire me? I have a union rep that called me and tipped me off that he has been asking questions about contracts, plus it's obvious to the world we hate each other – it's embarrassing in fact. I just wish it were as obvious to everyone what a pathetic excuse for an editor and human being he is. No Liz don't worry about me. I'll survive somehow – I always have. And if Caldwell succeeds in firing me then it's not worth it any more anyway. I don't want to be here on his watch if he is calling the shots much longer. Don't waste a second feeling bad about getting a promotion.

In fact, let me know how I can help." Elizabeth listened as a gush of warm reassurance washed over her. Clark had slayed bigger and smarter dragons than Caldwell.

"OK…I guess I better go inside and tell Caldwell about MacDougal's seizure and that he is gonna have to wait for his story….you want to come with me?" asked Clark grinning. Elizabeth grinned back at him. She grabbed his hand and squeezed it. She had come clean and the air between her and Clark was clear.

"As future city editor – I advise you NOT to go in there and tell Caldwell anything right now. We better sit here and come up with a plan," said Elizabeth smiling.

A knock on the window startled them both. It was Richie Byrne. He was standing at the driver's side window and sweating profusely. It was his weight however, rather than exercise as the source of perspiration. Clark rolled down the window smiling.

"Hey guys. Caldwell is looking for you. I wouldn't go in right now though. Let him calm down or you'll take his head off," said Richie. Clark nodded.

"He is going to be even more pissed when I tell him our subject had a full on seizure during our interview and we are going to have to go back at some point…" Clark thought out loud.

"You don't have the story? Oh shit…we better think of something," said Richie, thinking hard. "Hey, I've got an idea – I just got off the phone with a source in Washington when I was checking out that medallion you found. Turns out that spot where you found the medallion might be a pretty significant military installation. Let's take a ride up there now and check it out, the three of us will team up on an expose feature and at least we won't return empty handed. I'll get in the back." And Richie Byrne jumped into the back seat of Clark Westfield's car.

"You just want to get out of the office and satisfy your history fetish," laughed Clark. "And I need an excuse to dodge Caldwell… Sure, let's take a ride. By the way, Richie, how was the source you spoke with? Is she doing ok?" jibed Clark as he made eye contact with Richie in the back seat. As old friends Clark knew the whole story and where Richie used to get his 'information'.

"Fuck off Westfield! I'm trying to save your old ass…" laughed Richie and the three of them turned onto the Garden State Parkway and headed North.

Clark slowed down around the sharp curve of Arden Road after looping through Tiorati circle. He was searching for the second eye level white sign that declared the area off the road restricted. The heavy green leaf color made finding the sign from the road difficult. Once the car slowed down the three reporters got out. Richie sipped on his water bottle, and Elizabeth stretched and struck several yoga poses. The air was heavy, thick and hot. Various birds and forest wildlife scurried and could be heard in the distance and close. Clark looked around. He looked at his colleagues. He was both proud and defeated at the same time.

"Ok guys, that's the trail," said Clark pointing at the faint gravel path through the woods leading straight up the hillside. "It's really steep but once it curves around that boulder the mine is only about 100 yards."

"Of course, there would have to be major road access for a site on this scale. I'm sure there is an alternative closed road for larger vehicles," observed Richie scanning the woods and talking to himself. The three colleagues started up the steep hillside single file. Clark led and Elizabeth was second and Richie Byrne lugged behind. As they turned right around the huge boulder at the top of the hill, they felt the first blast of cold air. Elizabeth looked at Clark surprised.

"That's the air from the mine," explained Clark. "It's going to get a lot colder as we go forward. That's going to keep happening and its air coming out of the mine." Elizabeth nodded and panted. Richie shook his head and looked down.

The three inched their way up to the main entrance of the cavernous structure. Clark stopped and stood at the water's edge. The 30 foot ceiling of the Bradley mine with its skylights stood ominously before them. "Well, this is it," said Clark.

"Wait a minute, the mine is flooded. There is just water here," said Richie Byrne, looking around.

"Yeah, we told you that several times Richie," said Elizabeth genuinely surprised that he was surprised.

"Yeah, I know that Ms. Cranford," replied Richie sarcastically. "So where is the cold air coming from if the mine is flooded, teacher? Not here clearly…"

"Holy shit you are right!" exclaimed Clark. "But how could that be? Why is that happening and where is the cold air coming from?"

"She was right…." Richie Byrne's voice trailed off.. "She said there would be an alternative entrance. She said they all have alternative entrances. Guys – there is another entrance to this mine. And it's a legit Continuity of Government Civil Defense Bunker. We have to find it. Let's go this way!" Richie walked off to the right of the entrance and trudged through the woods.

"I really hope that source wasn't just trying to get us lost," thought Clark. "Scorned lovers have been known to do much worse." Elizabeth rolled her eyes and followed Clark and Richie along the right side of the mine over what would be the roof if it were a conventional building. "There!" exclaimed Richie as he pointed forward. The three colleagues could see two railroad ties standing vertically 10 yards apart tied together with a sagging steel cable. A metal sign with writing that had washed off long ago in decades of rainstorms hung flaccidly in the middle. Richie started scratching at the dirt with his shoes. "Here it is!" he shouted as Clark and Elizabeth came over to see what he was looking at. A square metal door was revealed under the debris, set in a larger rectangular concrete slab. "This must be one of the entrances, guys give me a hand with this," said Richie, straining.

"Rich, do you not see the imprint in the metal door that says, "Property of U.S. Government – No Trespassing?" asked Elizabeth sternly.

"Don't worry about it – this probably hasn't been opened in at least 50 years Liz. This site isn't even on the list of active COG sites," said Richie as he strained to heave up the heavy metal door.

"Are you sure this is a good idea?" Clark wondered aloud as the steel door fell on its opposite side revealing what looked like a 36-inch diameter concrete pipe shaft with metal ladder rungs molded into the side. Before he could protest further, Richie had already disappeared down the metal ladder. The light from his cell phone flashlight flickered below. Elizabeth and Clark looked at each other not knowing what to do. Elizabeth sighed loudly.

"Clark, I'm not going down there…" but before she could protest further, Clark was balancing himself on the top metal ladder rungs.

"Show me how the light on my cell phone works Liz please," said Clark as he handed her his phone.

"You're serious? You don't even know how to turn on your cell phone flashlight and you are going down into a flooded mine that is pitch dark…for what reason exactly?" protested Elizabeth.

"Because if Richie is right and no one has seen this in fifty years and it's really a government bunker - then we've got a story, and this must be what MacDougal was talking about so I'm going down. You want to stay up here and keep watch fine but don't come down unless you tell us. We might need someone up here to help us out. Ha!" said Clark as Elizabeth glanced around worriedly.

Clark descended down the ladder though a shoulder tight concrete shaft. Some of the ladder rungs creaked and crumbled under his weight. Numbers were pressed into the concrete at each rung. At the 84th rung he felt solid rock ground beneath him. He waved his cell phone around at the brown rock walls. It was jagged sandstone that had been chipped away to form a large tunnel about eight feet high and four feet wide. Clark's cell phone didn't provide much light. There was no sign of Richie.

"Rich? Where did you go?" called Clark. It suddenly occurred to him that if his cell phone light turned off, he would be in total pitch darkness.

"Walk down and to the right," he heard Richie yell. Despite being nervous of leaving the safety of the ladder, Clark slowly inched his way forward with his hand stabilizing and trailing against the damp rock wall. As he got about 40 feet a large dim pool of light illuminated the floor. Two more steps and the tunnel made an abrupt turn. Clark turned to see an enormous room-sized cavern, lit by utility lights behind metal mesh wires protecting the glass from breaking. The floor of the cavern had a perfectly built set of steps in masonry concrete. The room was as big as the living room of an average house. Two large gray metal desks were bolted into the rock floor on which three massive ringed binders sat. One was marked "Continuity of

Government Protocol Manual A," the second said "Military and Civilian Inclusion Ledger, Identification Codes and Roster" and the third said "Weapons and Essential Supply Inventory Ledger and Bunker Schematics,". On the left wall, was a large yellow painted metal sign with the three-triangle radiation symbol and the words ``Decontamination Unit" over a large arrow pointing down a descending tunnel. The right wall had a massive metal sign with copious amounts of writing under the words "BLAST DOOR OPENING/CLOSING INSTRUCTIONS." The far wall opposite Clark had a massive steel door, bigger than a bank vault door. A large steering wheel sized metal ring was in the center which seemed to be a pressurized doorknob. Caution markers and yellow hazard stickers were in every nook and cranny of the door, and the hinges were almost six feet in length extending to the middle. Richie stood at the two heavy metal desks and started flipping through the first binder marked PROTOCOLS.

"Holy Shit Clark.." said Richie without looking up. "This is a gold mine Clark! A goddam gold mine…!" Something about being deep underground made it natural to default to a whisper.

"I think I read this was an iron mine rich…" replied Clark, still looking around.

"It's actually neither," Richie turned around and faced Clark directly. "Clark this is the check in room for a Continuity of Government site. I've never seen one…and I was on a nuclear submarine dammit! This is where key government officials and other strategic VIPS would go if there was a nuclear war. HO-Ly Shit!…always read about them but never seen one."

"So that sign that says blast doors – that's what they mean by blast?" asked Clark pointing to the doors.

"Yes – we won't be able to open those. They might be 24 inches thick. They would be opened by a military officer if we went to Defcon 3. Then armed officers from each military branch would channel people into the next room where presumably there would be food, supplies, communications equipment and a hell of a lot more protocol binders…" said Richie while still thoughtfully glancing around and inspecting the room.

"More protocol binders? Why so many?" Clark asked sarcastically.

"Well, we were taught there would be bunker rules which would describe the chain of command, and everything else needed including critical information of re-emergence and re-building instructions." Richie said still in a stream of thought.

"Rebuilding instructions..?" asked Clark incredulously.

"Well, everything on the top side would be destroyed…or most of it anyway. You'd have to decide where to start to rebuild – what gets saved, what can't be saved, what to do with any survivors…etc. It wouldn't be pretty," Richie shook his head.

"What is up with that decontamination sign?" Clark said, pointing to the radiation symbol.

"Oh – all decon units have to be before the blast doors because you can't let people in if they have radiation on their clothes or shoes or had been exposed. But realistically there is no avoiding it if there were any explosions. Plus, if New York got hit with any of the later thermonuclear devices this area is too close to be of any help. People would have to evacuate long before any bombs went off and seal in here tight because we are less than 40 miles from where ground zero would be. Wow this is a real living artifact from the Cold War. This could be a museum!" Riche smiled with the pride of a boy who just discovered an endless supply of candy.

"How did you turn on these overhead lights?" asked Clark as he motioned up at the protected ceiling lights.

"Oh, there is a lever on the wall, and it looks like they are routed to those ancient batteries over there. Those are supposed to have a shelf life of 200 years. If people have to get here in a hurry, they don't want the lights not to work." Richie explained.

"So, sites like these…" Clark was interrupted as Richie finished his sentence for him.

"Were all over the country in case we were ever under attack, and this one seems like a pretty important one. Some were big enough and outfitted to hold the high command or even the president – the idea was to make sure we had a functioning government in case we took heavy casualties in Washington or at key military bases. These locations were part of the internal PR campaign that kept us thinking we could win a nuclear war. It was places like this that let us lie to ourselves. We all bought that myth in one way or another…and it made us do terrible things." Richie's eyes filled with tears and his voice trailed off.

"Let's get back up to the surface buddy…Elizabeth is probably worried about us, and we can always come back," said Clark who was now eager to get back up to ground level. Richie looked at him and nodded, then turned and took one of the enormous binders marked PROTOCOLS and walked past Clark down the passageway towards the ladder leaving Clark alone in the room. Clark looked around one last time and muttered to himself – "Why would MacDougal bring him *here*?" The question nagged at him as climbed up the steel ladder rungs behind his colleague.

Chapter 6

Sean Caldwell looked at the three reporters seated in his office with contempt and rage. The parole hearing for Joseph MacDougal was a few days away and his plans for a section leading deep dive feature into one of the most violent crimes Northern New Jersey had ever seen were all but impossible as the three reporters sitting across from his desk explained that no interview had taken place in the state prison with the murderer. Caldwell made no attempt to hide his disgust. His face was flushed and red, and his tone was direct and adversarial.

"So let me get this straight," said the editor slowly. "You two went to Trenton State Prison after I arranged an interview with the warden of one of their inmates for a major Sunday feature pegged to his upcoming parole hearing, you didn't complete the interview, then instead of telling me about the delay, you met this guy in the parking lot (he pointed at Richie Byrne) and spent the bulk of yesterday wandering around up in the woods – and now we have…. NOTHING?"

Richie Byrne interrupted the silence: "Sean, we gotta do a story on the COG bunker, it's fascinating and will be really interesting… "

"Enough!" shot Caldwell. "Nobody cares about civil defense bunkers and Cold War nostalgia! They care about the fact that a mother has to appear at a parole hearing next Tuesday and explain why the sick bastard that assaulted and killed her 7-year-old son should stay in jail – THAT'S our story! Nothing else! It's bad enough that you guys fucked up this interview – its frankly insulting that you are trying to make a case that an abandoned shelter up in the woods has any merit as news. Are you people serious? What the hell am I gonna do about Sunday's piece?" The editor was fuming.

"We didn't fuck anything up Sean," said Clark in a low measured voice. "The guy had a seizure – which means we simply have to go back and interview him before Friday. I can do that tomorrow. I can interview the boy's mother Friday as well. Stop acting like it's the end of the world."

"Elizabeth can interview the boy's mother with you. And I better have an entire story on my desk by Friday midnight," said the editor, raising his voice.

"Right…or let me guess…I'm fired?" challenged Clark. Elizabeth shot him a glance and Richie turned to avoid eye contact. "Listen Sean – I know field work is both unfamiliar and challenging to guys like you that never really worked a beat – but for those of us that have been doing a long time this is normal and you get through the obstacles."

"You know, for a smug dinosaur, you are still showing up here empty handed and where I come from that's cause – as in cause for firing," said Caldwell challenging Clark right back. The two men sat with eyes locked until Richie Byrne broke the silence.

"Well, it sounds like we all have a lot of work to do…Liz, Clark, you'd better get back on the phone with the warden and it looks like I'll have to do some research with Washington about those bunkers in the mine…." And he abruptly got up and started to exit as Clark and Elizabeth followed him.

"Sure Richie…you get on that story," said Caldwell, not breaking his stare at Clark. "And tell her hello while you're at it," he added sarcastically. Richie paused a minute and realized it was a dig from Caldwell letting him know that he knew of his liaisons at the Pentagon.

The three reporters stood quietly in a small area in front of Elizabeth's desk talking in hushed whispers. Clark fumbled through his emails on his phone to find the address for the department of corrections communications office and started to type an email requesting another interview with Joseph MacDougal. Elizabeth put an email up on her screen that was from their editor with the name, address and phone number of the Dellla Russo boy's mother along with the website she had set up that served both as a memorial to her dead son and an advocacy tool. The text in the email was a message instructing Elizabeth to call the woman and conduct the interview. She turned her screen so Clark could see the writing.

"I'm not going there without you Clark, I don't care what Caldwell says," she said softly.

Clark stared at the computer screen. The atmosphere was heavy. It had the urban charm of degraded industrial carpets, fluorescent overhead lighting and the gasp of failing air conditioning that made working in New Jersey in July unbearable. Richie Byrne spoke first.

"Look guys, I don't know what you think but something is up here that we need to figure out. The fact that the COG bunker is there is interesting enough on its own to warrant coverage, but the fact that MacDougal sent you there must be significant. I don't know how or what the connection is yet but there's something under the surface here and we need to find out what it is. I know you guys think I want an excuse to get back in touch with Kelly but honestly that's not it. I never saw a site like the one we discovered yesterday, and I was on a nuclear submarine for years!" His enthusiasm and intrigue were tangible.

"Well, if Clark can get back into the prison for an interview, he can just ask him…" said Elizabeth with a shrug.

"Look Rich, I think you are right that the expansive bunkers up there beg investigation and coverage – and I'm not going to judge you for making a trip to Washington, believe me I know you well enough. But I don't know that the two are connected… You don't know MacDougal, he is just a crazy old psychopath and that's what crazy people do, they lose control, they fuck with your head, they confuse you..its all part of his act. You go do your story and just remember to be careful as old wounds are like wet paint…some things never heal or wash off." Clark patted Richie on the shoulder affectionately. Richie nodded and fist bumped Clark, then disappeared down the hall. Elizabeth closed her computer and grabbed her purse.

"Come on Clark, you and I have an interview to do," she said, grabbing his elbow. She could feel that he was somewhat fragile. Even though Clark had been in many more difficult spots with stories throughout his career, the stress was starting to wear on him and show his age.

"Yes, madam editor!" Clark said with a smile. Elizabeth shot him a look of contempt, then broke into a smile. They left the newsroom and got into Elizabeth's car and headed to the Della Russo house.

Richie pulled his gray Toyota Camry into the farthest parking spot in the rest area on Rt. 95. The seedy parking lot was badly in need of paving and striping, littered with garbage and several seagulls stood aimlessly in the summer heat watching trash blow around at random. The dilapidated building was the archetypical disgusting highway rest room, painted beige cinder blocks that formed a box around a men's and women's restrooms that smelled of ammonia and mold. He got out of his car and sat at the picnic table that adorned the grass oval dividers. The heat was scorching. He could see the outline of the Pentagon in the distance through the summer haze. While he was excited about the story he was working on, his anxiety at seeing Lt. Col. Kelly Pram was boiling inside his guts. Did he really want this story or was he opening old wounds and sitting down on wet paint as Clark had said. A hand touched his shoulder.

"You've gained some weight," said the soft female baritone voice. Lt. Col. Pram sat on the opposite side of the picnic table.

"Nice to see you as well," replied Richie immediately feeling like it may have been a bad idea to agree to an in-person meeting. "I was surprised you asked to meet after hearing how upset you were on the phone the other day."

"Don't flatter yourself Rich," said Lt.Col Pram coldly. "You should be thanking me for saving your ass and I'm going to need you to do exactly as I say." He looked at her surprised and then realized that whatever she was about to say was very serious.

"I know you well enough that after we spoke the other day you would probably be going to explore that COG site," Lt. Col Pram explained. "And sure enough, like the creature of habit that you are, you went up there and entered the bunker, didn't you?" Richie nodded, unsure of how she knew or what she was getting at. "You tripped a sensor that gets activated when the bunker door is opened. I anticipated that you would do exactly that, so I went over to the signals wing and waited in the control room and when the signal came in, I told the commanding officer I had a technician in the field that was doing a routine maintenance check. He actually believed me and you're in the clear. You can thank me anytime." Lt. Pram sat and paused for a minute.

"Umm well, thanks. I guess some part of you still wants to look out for me?" said Richie mustering a smile. "Did you want to see me so you could thank me in person?"

Lt. Pram sighed. "No, you really are in love with yourself, aren't you? No, I needed to see you because the Harriman Mine sites are highly classified and have a really messy history."

"Glad to see they aren't the only ones with a messy past," said Richie in an attempt to add levity. "I'll only report what you want me to Kelly, you know that. But I'd love to do a feature series on Cold War planning and localize it a bit."

"You can't do it on the Harriman sites Rich.." She said with a serious expression. "You gotta leave this alone. I'll find something else interesting for you and make it worth the switch, but please, walk away from this one.." He could see that she was troubled by the warning she was giving him.

"Kel, you've never blocked me on a story before. I've already apologized for everything and if I could change the past I would but.."

"Oh god dammit Richie Byrne it's not always about you!" exclaimed the Lt. Col. ``You worked as a nuclear weapons technician in the Strategic Triad – you know damn well how sensitive these things can get. I didn't come here because I was dying to see you – I gladly just assumed never to see you again. I came here because I know how damn good a reporter you are and that you are going to keep digging, literally, until somebody inside the Pentagon sees you as a threat and takes action. STAY THE FUCK AWAY FROM HARRIMAN!" Lt. Col Pram's face was red, and she was clearly upset.

"OK….but you gotta tell me why," said Richie slowly.

"There are a few reasons," said Lt. Col Pram as her eyes looked far away onto the horizon at the Pentagon off in the distance. "First, you know who Averell Harriman was of course." Richie nodded as she continued. "Then you know that he helped FDR and Truman end World War 2, so he obviously was integral to the Manhattan project. That meant when he became ambassador to the Soviet Union, he was also the architect of the entire civil defense response during the Cold War. It also meant that all those abandoned mines up on his state park property got preferential treatment when it came to building bunkers. Think about it – you have a Continuity of Government bunker that you get to design yourself on land that your family used to own and only you have the maps and surveying of the network of mines? So needless to say, there is the official record of what's up in Harriman and then there is what is actually up there."

"OK, so there are some black sites – I won't report that. Plus, any money for those sites would be from a 50 year old defense budget – who cares?" interjected Richie.

"It's not the money Richie – of course no one cares what the government overspent outside the defense budget lines 50 years ago. It's what else you could do at a site and get away with if nobody knew about it…" Lt. Pram stopped for a moment and their eyes connected. Richie thought about Harriman state park with its network of lakes, the many cabins and dining halls around the campsites that were used in the summer by kids from New York City public schools, youth groups, special Olympics events, etcetera.

"So, amidst all the summer fun and decades of camp counselor's raging romances you had a fully operational cold war black site flourishing with programs nobody could know about?" asked Richie. "I'm still not seeing what the big deal is beyond nostalgic intrigue." He squinted with a confused look. There was clearly something she wasn't telling him.

"The Cassandra Unit was the command center for the MK Ultra program." Lt. Col Pram broke eye contact and they sat in silence for several seconds as she let the news sink in. "The COG bunker you found was an adjunct to the complex, but MK started…and ended..up in Harriman." Richie shook his head.

"No, Kel, you're wrong. Everyone knows MK Ultra started at various educational campuses and military base sites, mostly McGill University in Montreal and was a university based network of academics.."

"You're smarter than that Richie Byrne!" She cut him off mid-sentence. "That's the cover story and the one that came out in the Rockefeller congressional hearings in the 1970's. That's the comfortable version that's easy for the public to believe and avoids accountability for people like Averell Harriman and his cronies. MK Ultra started in the late 1950's and was fully operational for two decades, and it was run out of those mine sites in New York State. It carried out various missions and there were multiple problems and casualties. The LSD experiments have always been a distraction from the real truth which is that the CIA was domestically training assassins to carry out missions around the world. The one place they could operate without being disturbed was a COG bunker because nobody – especially the military, local police, local residents, whatever, would question anyone saying they were building a civil defense site."

"And the camps around all the lakes? Were they part of it also?" asked Richie, now completely intrigued by what he was hearing.

"Of course. They were full of people who were either being screened for the program or working in the program or actively carrying out missions. Many of them didn't even know they were being recruited. Many were inner city students from New York City public schools who scored really high on standardized tests. They would be given a summer camp scholarship through the school system and go up to one of the lake camps where counselors that were actually intelligence staff could assess their aptitudes. Some got enrolled in additional modules, some got sent home, some graduated to be operatives," explained Lt. Pram in a matter-of-fact tone.

"I don't believe it – you couldn't keep something that size a secret. Those camps up there and those lakes, they had thousands of kids each summer and you want me to believe that over five or six decades no one up there talked? That doesn't add up Kel…" Richie shook his head.

"You assume everyone knew why they were there," continued Lt. Col Pram "It's not like a bus pulled up and they all sang welcome to the CIA around the campfire while roasting marshmallows. Use that fat head of yours Richie Byrne – you were on a submarine and didn't even know what your orders were until after your mission sometimes. Most if not all of the recruits up in the Harriman MK Ultra had no idea why they were there or what was happening. They were given flattery, encouragement, affection and accommodations that they weren't getting at home, all the while thinking they were simply escaping the ghetto on an academic scholarship."

"And some wound up activated on missions?" asked Richie. Lt. Col Pram nodded her head. "And when you say casualties…..what kind of casualties are you referring to?" he asked.

"Well, that should be obvious – do you think every lost hiker really got lost? Do you think every time someone drowned in one of the lakes it's because another kid couldn't swim? I'm sure half of the suicide cases in the Harriman police files were some MK Ultra event. You know how messy that program was." She looked at him with a stern look, Richie sighed.

"What I know is this," he paused before speaking. "It has long been known that the government did terrible things with the MK Ultra program through the CIA, which they have admitted to in congressional hearings and books. They've even settled lawsuits out of court, so none of that is news. But if you are telling me that a massive state park 30 miles north of New York City was set up and designed by government agents as a recruitment and training site to feed the program and there are still COG bunkers up there that will be interesting to the residents of New Jersey at the very least, and I'm damn well gonna report it!"

"You, if anybody should know what you are up against and to leave this alone," said Lt. Col Pram with a look of concern. "I know how hardheaded you are, and I know that you are going to want to run with this, and as much I may loathe you and the havoc you wrecked in my life, I'm trying to stop you by warning you. PLEASE RICHIE! DROP THIS!"

A long silence ensued between them. "You really loathe me?" he asked her tenderly.

"No…," said the colonel. A tear escaped her eyelid, and she gathered her composure and walked away. Richie Byrne didn't watch her go.

Elizabeth pulled up outside the house in Westvale where Isabella Della Russo lived. Clark sat in the passenger seat motionless. Elizabeth looked at him and realized he was deep in thought and somewhere else mentally.

"You ok?" she asked. "Is it the thought of how uncomfortable this interview is going to be or is it all the shit that Caldwell is throwing at you back at the office? Listen we will find a way around all this Clark, let's just go do our job for now." She was trying to be nurturing. Despite the age difference Clark had started to feel like a peer as their careers progressed, and she remembered how much he had defended her in her early years in the workplace as she now found herself doing the same for him. He looked at the front door of the house they were about to walk up to.

"Liz, it's tough," Clark tried to explain. "This story started when I was 8 years old – when I first found the case files. It's what made me a reporter. It's been with me my entire life. It's like a bad dream I can't get rid of. The fact that it's an opportunity for Caldwell to try to fire me isn't just the height of irony, I almost want it to happen. Plus, I've sat across from the man who killed this lady's son, but I never actually could bring myself to interview her – and I'm sure there is some resentment on her end that I didn't." His voice trailed off as he was welling with emotion.

"What would you have told me if I was the one in the passenger seat saying what you're saying now?" Liz asked gently. Clark smiled.

"I would tell you to get your ass up and do your job," he replied jovially. Elizabeth got out of the car and walked up the walkway towards the front door. Clark trailed behind her slowly and timidly. A woman in her late 70's answered the door. It was Isabella

Della Russo, the deceased boy's mother. She beckoned for Elizabeth to come in and held the storm door open for her. As Clark approached Ms. Della Russo met his gaze and her smile disappeared. She politely held the door for Clark as they entered the house.

Elizabeth and Clark sat on opposite ends of the couch as Ms. Della Russo sat in an armchair directly across from them. A tray with two teacups and a pitcher of tea was arranged on a coffee table in the center of the room. Despite the searing July heat Ms. Della Russo wore a heavy sweater around her shoulders and looked frail and bloodless. She was a dignified ancient prune-like woman that appeared to harbor both a deep wisdom and pain – the kind of expression a parent wears when they've buried a child over 40 years ago.

"Thank you for agreeing to meet with us Ms. Della Russo," said Elizabeth politely and gently. She felt she needed to say something to break the heavy silence as Clark sat motionless in a trance-like state.

"You're welcome," said the old woman in a barely audible whisper. "How can I help you?" Her stare was intent.

"Well, with the parole hearing coming up we know that you have to appear before the parole board and give a victim's statement, which you've had to do in the past so we thought we could talk about what it is you want the public to know about that and how difficult it is.."

"It's not difficult at all.." said Ms. Della Russo, still staring intently.

"I'm sorry? I'm not sure I follow.." said Elizabeth as she opened her notebook and began to write. Clark continued to sit motionless on the couch as he and Ms. Della Russo stared at one another.

"Telling a parole tribunal that a man should be in jail for murdering my son is by no means difficult. Telling them how wonderful he was and how full of life he was and how he went out one day and never came home because of this sick twisted maniac's actions isn't difficult. What's difficult is that our society still gives him enough of the benefit of the doubt that it's even a consideration he comes up for parole. What's difficult is that since his death I advocated and got a law passed that mandates life without parole for child murderers who also commit a sex crime, but it doesn't apply to him – only those who came after. I'm happy to appear every few years so future parents don't have to do the same thing for their lost children," said Ms. Della Russo sternly.

"So, do you see your work on behalf of all future victims? We hope by reporting the story to support you in that effort, its important people know not just how wonderful your son was but how your life's work since then has been to help others…." Elizabeth was trying to sound supportive, but it was coming across as transparent.

"Perhaps it's a countermeasure to those who may try to humanize him," she said, looking at Clark coldly. Elizabeth looked at Clark then back at the old woman realizing there was no surmounting the enormous tension that hung over the room.

"Ms. Della Russo, let me explain.." Clark said in an exasperated tone. The old woman cocked her head as if she genuinely wanted to watch Clark squirm through what he had to say. "I'm not going to hide or deny the fact that I was an opportunistic young reporter and used the first interview I got with him to be seen at the paper. I got the interview because my father was his defense attorney as you know, but I did it because people needed to never forget how dangerous this guy was. That may have been young and foolish and selfish of me, but believe me I would never humanize that monster…never.."

Elizabeth broke the silence. "We would like to know what you want the readers to know about your advocacy efforts while we illustrate your strength all these years going to all these parole hearings." Her statement did nothing to unlock the icy stare the old woman had locked onto Clark.

"What did your father tell you about the case?" she asked Clark, ignoring Elizabeth and locking her intense stare with Clark.

"Well, to be honest, I found the legal case files when I was about 8 years old in our garage after I knocked them over, so I saw all the pictures and I read the police reports, the coroner's reports. I was pretty shaking up, and over the years I kept asking my dad how he could defend such a terrible person. He explained it was a guilty plea, so he was making sure everything went the way it was supposed to in court and he wasn't trying to get anyone off the hook…" explained Clark cathartically.

"And your father told you my son had been sexually assaulted?" asked the old woman with her steely stare.

"Yes, and I saw the pictures," explained Clark. "Listen Ms. Della Russo, I have no interest in mitigating or explaining anything this man did – I just think it's important people know the impact these events had.."

"You have no idea the impact these events had on me or elsewhere," said the old woman sternly. "What did Joseph MacDougal tell you when you interviewed him?"

"Honestly, he didn't tell me much…the first time he just screamed at me and when we went to see him earlier this week, he just suddenly had a seizure so we don't really have very much. Listen, I'm not trying to portray any false empathy here. I can't imagine what you or your family have been through. I'm a reporter trying to do my job, and this has been a major story for the duration of my life – that's really all I'm trying to do." Clark's tone was contrite. He was truly sorry if his early interviews of Joseph MacDougal had caused her any stress and he was embarrassed that his finagling of that first prison interview had come across as opportunistic. Deep down he knew it was, and he saw this experience with Ms. Della Russo as a way of making amends – but it seemed she wasn't buying it.

"So, he told you nothing about his version of events?" asked the old woman.

Clark shook his head no.

"And your father never told you anything beyond the case files?" asked the old woman again. Clark shook his head no again.

"Then I'd like to thank you both for coming and for reporting on my son's murder," said Ms. Della Russo. And just like that she rose from the armchair slowly with visible arthritis and opened the front door while beckoning for them to leave with her arm. Clark got up and grabbed Elizabeth's elbow and nodded a thank you and pulled her out the front door with him.

They drove away in silence and headed down Westvale Avenue in town. This was the town Clark had grown up in. He had ridden his bicycle down these exact streets past these exact houses as a child just like little Anthony Della Russo. As the car approached the Catholic Church in the center of town, Clark motioned for Elizabeth to turn right into the parking lot. Elizabeth, still reeling from the hostile interview and sensitive to how much it must have torn up Clark, did as he suggested and drove into the vast parking lot. At one end was an elementary school with a 1950's architecture of ugly industrial brick, at the other end was a post Vatican 2 church that was constructed like a five-point star rather than a classic cathedral box with a pointy roof. The sprawling church was surrounded by manicured grass fields and a brook dotted with willow trees. Clark motioned for Elizabeth to stop the car. He got out and walked closer to a statue of an angel. Elizabeth got out in the July heat and walked up beside him, not sure what to say.

"Well," she said, trying to break the tension. "That went well, and Caldwell will be thrilled." Clark ignored her attempt at humor and stood fixated on the statue. Elizabeth then realized that the Statue of the Angel was the memorial shrine to the murdered boy, Anthony Della Russo, complete with his name and birth and death dates and an inscription "Now Forever With the Angels" chiseled into the marble. Above the carved inscription was a ceramic oval the size of a football with the little boy's portrait photograph in the veneer. He was in his scout uniform; it was the same picture the paper had run dozens of times in the news coverage over the years. Clark stood fixated on it as

Elizabeth tried to awkwardly figure out what to do or say next.

"Look," said Clark as he pointed at the oval portrait.

"Yeah he is beautiful…such an angel.." said Elizabeth.

"No, look," said Clark pointing again.

"OK what am I looking at?" asked Elizabeth bewildered.

Clark squatted down and got really close to the statue, putting his

index finger at a spot on the oval portrait where perfect young

seven-year-old boy in his scout uniform wore a shirt adorned with

various patches. One of which was a blue triangle inside a yellow

circle, just like the medallion Clark had found.

Chapter 7

Clark looked at Richie Byrne glancing nervously around the National Mall. The Washington Monument was far to their right, the Lincoln Memorial to their left. They sat facing East at the midpoint path as Richie watched various joggers, young couples pushing strollers, vacationing families from the midwest and Asian tourists sail by in a carousel of recreational activities. All oblivious to the confluence of darker forces parked in offices around the town making life and death decisions on people far away and our quality of life. A toddler and his parents who were flying a kite seemed the perfect metaphor for an exuberant joyous average American family who had no idea the cost of their freedoms or the malicious intent that ran concurrent to American idealism.

"Why are you sweating?" asked Clark.

"I'm not sweating," replied Richie, then realized he indeed was covered in beads of salty liquid. "OK, well, I'm sitting here thinking I can't believe you talked me into driving down here and meeting Kelly and that I don't know if I'm really up for this meeting."

"OK, first of all you said you met up with Kelly already so this shouldn't be that big a deal," persuaded Clark. "Plus, she is our only source that will help us make any progress on this. We are journalists Richie; our highest calling is accessing those who know and want to talk. People like Lt. Col. Kelly Pram need men like us on the outside that serve as a checkpoint for what the government is doing at all times. Plus, you said you wanted to write something on the bunker up in Harriman anyway, and that will be a blockbuster piece, so I don't know what you are so wound up about…"

"Because Clark, it's REALLY complicated with me and Kelly!" interrupted Richie. "While the whole episode is something that I would really like to forget and worked very hard to move past, the fucked-up thing is that there are still underlying feelings that make no sense. I don't need a story this bad, believe me…"

A mature woman with graying hair in sweatpants and a T-shirt walked up. Her hair was pulled back in a bun, and she wore sunglasses and an action sports bra she would wear in a snowboarding competition. Around her waist was a pink Velcro fanny pack that looked like it hadn't been washed since 1983.

"Hello boys. I see you are both doing a great job of blending in...." said Lt. Col Pram sarcastically. Both men looked surprised that they had not seen her approaching and that she had caught them unaware.

"Oh! Kelly! I didn't recognize you without your uniform," said Richie trying to be polite.

"You've seen me when I'm not wearing my uniform before," replied Lt. Col Pram dryly. "Are you going to introduce me to Mr. Westfield?" Lt. Col Pram extended her hand for Clark to shake. Clark accepted, slightly surprised that she knew his name and immediately realized she was letting him know that she had found it out prior to the meeting on her own.

"Military intelligence officers frequently use the introduction spoiler technique to throw the subject off balance and imply they are in a superior position of knowledge. You wear it well Lt. Col., and I'm pleased to make your acquaintance," said Clark, smiling and extending his hand.

"Yes well, you were with Richie and another colleague when you tripped the sensor in the Harriman bunker, so we logged you into our facial recognition app and that confirmed it was you on the bench with scribe Byrne over here," explained Kelly Pram.

"You got a team on us? Are we being watched?" Richie asked, glancing around nervously.

"No, you idiot," snapped Lt. Col Kelly Pram. "I didn't let anyone know that we had met or that you were coming. Are you crazy? I told you I had to do some fast maneuvering to make sure you didn't get caught or arrested after the bunker breach. I also knew deep down that once I told you of some of the clandestine history of the site you'd be back....despite warnings...and like clockwork here you are."

"If it's any consolation, I convinced him to call this meeting," Clark butted in. "First of all, lieutenant, thank you for agreeing to meet – this is of course off the record and confidential, and thank you for the help so far. I have a broken link I need to establish, and I thought you would be one of the few people that could help. Can we talk about MK Ultra?"

"I don't know what I could tell you that isn't well documented in public record testimony and well researched books Mr. Westfield," Pram said in her steady firm tone. "The only real new information here is that Harriman State Park in New York was an operational site for many of the activities and research that were described in the Rockefeller senate hearings that started in 1975. The ethical violations and abuses are all well described, and President Gerald Ford issued a blanket apology and admission of CIA abuses that lead to both oversight and reform, including meeting directly with the families of those hurt by the experiments, the most famous being the Olson family who lost their father Frank Olson. I'm not sure there is much more to the whole thing – even after the documentation was made public the physical sites where the research took place are redacted to this day. Assuming Harriman is one of the sites, the current redaction means it would be a national security violation to report it. You're smarter than to violate national secrecy laws for a cold war nostalgia piece in a regional newspaper Mr. Westfield, but I hope you wouldn't be so short sighted and eager to manipulate Mr. Byrne into doing so and taking the fall." Her tone was even and commanding with a very clear directive.

"Lieutenant, I have no intention of violating national security and frankly MK Ultra and the cold war don't interest me very much," Clark said in an equally even and measured tone. "I'm reporting on a man who is convicted of murdering a seven year old boy and he is coming up for a parole hearing.."

"I don't think you'll have to worry about him being granted parole," interrupted Lt. Col. Pram.

"Well, maybe not, but I do need to know why he sent us up to the Harriman mine which turned out to be the bunker," explained Clark. "I also need to know why he hid his body up there and why he had a seizure when I showed him the medallion marker for the entrance.."

"You showed him the COG symbol? Good God…." Lt. Col Pram shook her head.

"Yes, I did! Why are you shaking your head? Why is that a big deal?" asked Clark. "Where is all this connected and what does that murder in 1973 have to do with these secret CIA programs and the

COG bunkers? That's what I am trying to find out. That's what we came down here to ask you."

Lt. Kelly Pram sat silent for several seconds then let out a sigh. "Well, I don't know the answer to what you are asking. A conspiracy theorist would wager an educated guess that your convicted child murderer, Joseph MacDougal, was likely one of the thousands of research subjects that were given massive amounts of LSD, mescaline or other very powerful drugs – he may even have been a volunteer – and that lead to some psychosis that resulted in violent behavior. But it's irresponsible and insensitive to the victim's family to report that because there is no way to prove any of it so you would just be pedaling some pretty gut-wrenching propaganda, and I'm sure you want the world to believe you are too good a reporter to do that."

"But what if there was a way to prove it?" asked Clark. "What if I'm able to get another interview with him and he admits it? There must be a list somewhere of everyone that was enrolled in the experimentation program…"

"Oh, sure there were lists, there was extensive documentation," Lt. Col. Pram affirmed in a sing-song voice. "But the program was stopped in 1973 and all records were destroyed. Remember, Vietnam was raging, the Pentagon Papers had proven the government knew they were lying to us about the war, and Watergate was heating up and there was a general panic that anything on paper that could make the government look bad or guilty could potentially cause a collapse or a civil war. Then CIA director Gottlieb ordered the destruction of massive amounts of documentation from the origins of the Vietnam mess to bioweapons to protection of high ranking captured Nazi scientists – it all went in the shredder and the furnace. MK Ultra was considered one on a long list of major initiatives that the public simply couldn't handle for its own good. This was all entered into the congressional record and reported on in the hearings in 1975-6. That whole congressional investigation was spurred by a series of New York Times articles after interviews with people claiming to be informants. I bet that's a story you wish you broke at your New Jersey paper Mr. Westfield." Her tone was biting and purposely hurtful.

"Yeah, I do wish I broke that story but I was three years old," Clark replied sarcastically. "But the bigger issue, Lt. Col., is that the government doesn't get to hurt its citizens, deny it happened, shred evidence and then shrug an apology when they get caught. If this little boy was murdered because the CIA's alleged research was the catalyst for psychotic behavior, then that means it's crucial material evidence in a trial, certainly in a parole hearing and in congressional accountability hearings…I'm surprised I have to point that out to you. So, while you may think this chapter is long laid to rest because President Ford did a White House apology photo op and there has been some thriller novels written and academic ethical guidelines adopted for experiments – there is a family up in New Jersey who deserve answers about the senseless murder of their son and a man appearing before a parole board who has the right to defend himself. Who cares what the government did 40 years ago that it already admitted to? I'm asking, on behalf of the lives that are still hurting over this, that you simply see if there is anything anywhere that documents Joseph MacDougal in a situation that could have led to violent behavior. That's all." As Clark finished speaking, Lt. Col Pram simply stared back at him. She removed her sunglasses and stared down at the dirt path that ran on both sides of the mall.

"I wouldn't even know where to begin to look," she sighed. "I also don't know what good would come of it if we did find anything."

Richie elbowed Clark and got his attention. He gave him a look that men give when they are instigating a manipulative action and need you to go along with it.

"Clark, why not take a walk and go get a snow cone or something? I'd like to talk here with Kelly for a while. I don't think she can help us." Richie nodded as he spoke. Clark stood up from the bench and made eye contact with the Lt. Col, slightly bowing his head in nonverbal gesture of respect and walked towards the Lincoln Memorial. When he had been walking five minutes his cell phone buzzed with a text message from Richie that read: "Go home and leave me here. I'll take a train home. I've got an idea, but I need to be alone with Kelly. I'll call when I can."

Clark smirked and typed back "LOL Sure thing partner. Enjoy."

Elizabeth sat at the head of a large table in the newspaper conference room. Seated randomly with bored looks on their faces were several college interns. They were from the graphics design and digital publishing department of Rutgers University, a department and field of academic study that had not existed when Elizabeth Cranford and Clark Westfield had matriculated through the university decades ago.

"Elizabeth I'm not sure you included an agenda in your digital invite," said a 20-year-old woman as she waved her phone in the air. Her hair had pink streaks that made her look like a toy skunk you would win in a boardwalk game. Her cheekbone had a diamond rhinestone simply adhered to the skin, perhaps held in place by a spike buried under the flesh making a one-sided piercing. Bolts in the face with fake diamonds on them seemed to be appearing more and more among the interns.

"When I set a meeting, your job is to show up and take notes and instructions. Where is your notepad?" asked Elizabeth with a steely gaze. Something had shifted in recent years among the college interns – they felt completely at ease challenging superiors with complete abandon. Elizabeth had fired one a month ago, sat two others down for warning about insubordinate behavior and now she was being confronted about how she worded a meeting invite.

"I just think it's better for everyone if we know what the meeting is about. That's all. And I take notes on my phone," said the pink haired intern without looking up from her phone screen. Elizabeth was both baffled and disgusted. She decided that she would give the assignment out to the group and then give the pink haired intern a stern warning about workplace attitude.

"We have a major feature coming up next week and we want to make it look terrific, both in print and online. We are going to put some promotion money behind it, the newspaper's PR office will probably pitch television stations to see if they want to interview Clark about the case. We want to initiate lots of comments in the discussion section and social media," Elizabeth was interrupted by the pink skunk.

"I'm sorry, what is this? What is the story? Who is Clark?" she said again without looking up.

"Clark Westfield is one of the paper's iconic reporters and one of the best known in the field of journalism. He has a story coming in next week about the upcoming parole hearing for a murderer in a pretty famous New Jersey case. But I wouldn't expect you to know that as you are probably too busy on your phone," said Elizabeth coldly while shooting the intern a stern look.

"Oh ok, I get it you want a murder feature marquis, and you want it to grab eyeballs, ok I can do that." The intern rose from her chair as she was talking, turned and was out the door of the conference room before she said her last word. Elizabeth sat at the head of the conference table, visibly perplexed and calmly trying to think of a next move that would show the other seated interns her disapproval at a depth they would never forget.

"Ms. Cranford, I have an idea," said a young man seated to her left as he meekly raised his hand as if he were in elementary school.

"For those of you who have decided to stay for the duration of the meeting, I would like to discuss layouts options." Elizabeth said to the rest of the group. The nervous eyeballs around the table avoided contact with the fierce woman at the head of the room. No one spoke.

"No one has any suggestions?" Elizabeth asked. The young man raised his hand again timidly.

"What if we do a gallery with pictures of the victim?" he asked in a meek voice.

"This murder was one of the biggest news stories in Bergen County in the last 50 years," seared Elizabeth. "Everyone knows what the victim looks like – there's even a shrine to him back at the local church with his portrait and everything. We need a new angle. They know what the perpetrator looks like also, his picture was everywhere. I don't want an updated photo of him as he doesn't deserve to be seen in his present state after his seven-year-old victim didn't have the privilege to live…" her voice trailed off. The case was always upsetting to her. No matter how many years had passed and how many times she had read about it or worked on tangential coverage the reality of what happened in Joseph MacDougal's basement was where she usually had to stop herself from thinking about the case any further.

"Ok everyone come back to me with ideas and mockups please – in 48 hours," Elizabeth said and dismissed the group. She sat alone at the conference table as the young staff filed out through the door. As the last intern left the pink skunk walked back in and stood next to Elizabeth.

"Ms. Cranford? I have an idea," she said with bold indifference.

"You left the meeting early before I could dismiss you," said Elizabeth who was now even more furious that she had returned and wanted private attention. "You need to understand that you report to a supervisor around here and you don't get to just.."

"Here take a look at this," interrupted the girl as she showed her the laptop computer turning it towards Elizabeth. On the screen was a collage of pictures, many were of the victim at different ages. There were no pictures of the murderer and placeholder text was arranged in magazine style columns over an off-white background. An emphasized graphics display of shaded bars and dots were arranged wallpaper style under the main photographs. The victim's formal school portrait was centered, and the text columns rolled around it in an elegant arc. The mock layout was expertly arranged, eye-catching and the more Elizabeth stared at it, seemingly perfect.

"We need to put his scout portrait in the middle, I know you said to the others that you didn't want his school portrait, but everyone will know that picture and it gives it historical context. Then, I downloaded some other photos from the family's memorial and advocacy website. I guess we will have to ask the foundation for permission – I can handle that if you'd like. I did the bars and the circles, and they are supposed to be dots and dashes for Morse code. I thought it was a nice touch, do you like it?" There was no humility in this young woman's explanation.

"Morse code?" asked Elizabeth.

"Yes…you know the old communication code of dots and dashes? They used to use it for telegrams…"

"I know what Morse code is, thank you," said Elizabeth, getting agitated. "But why on earth would you use that in the graphic layout? What does that have to do with anything?" Elizabeth shook her head as she asked. The streaked hair carefree and childlike intern tapped her finger in the middle of the screen on the boy's Scout portrait directly on a patch that had the triangle in a circle on it.

"What?" asked Elizabeth, baffled.

"That's the Boy Scout merit badge for Morse Code. He learned it in Boy Scouts," replied the intern smiling.

"You could earn a merit badge in Morse Code? How do you know this?" asked Elizabeth.

"Oh, I was a Girl Scout, and I took the Morse exam, it was really easy. They still teach it," she said,

"And you learned it? And that is why he has all these badges and patches on his shirt? Because each one is earned for learning a specific task… " Elizabeth sat thinking for a moment. The Merit Badge awarded for Morse code in the Boy Scouts was an identical logo to the Continuity of Government seal that she, Clark and Richie found at the mine. Something deep within told her that couldn't have been a coincidence…

✶✶

✶✶✶✶✶✶

The warden looked at Clark with a quizzical expression. The July heat made the stones of Trenton State prison façade as hot as an oven.

"You're back again? Seriously? After what happened last time?" asked the warden. "How much more do you need to know about this dirtbag anyway? He isn't going to get parole if that's what you're worried about." His tone rang with the all-consuming authority of a man who took joy keeping other men behind bars. Clark had driven to the prison without an appointment and didn't know whether MacDougal would even see him, especially after the seizure. The warden stared at Clark with his feet on his desk. His police baton aimlessly twirled defensive motions in the air. He picked up the phone and dialed the guard in the wing where MacDougal's cell was located.

"OK – he will take you over to a conference room on the pod," said the warden as he pointed to a deputy. "Like I said, there is no way this asshole gets parole, at least not on my watch, so I'm not the least bit worried about that. But Westfield, I should tell you that if you write some bleeding heart liberal horse shit about all the reasons this guy should get off I'll take it as personally offensive and I'll see it that your editor knows not only do you not care about public safety or a seven year old boy who was brutally assaulted and murdered, but that you are actively trying to undermine my position as warden. And well, I just couldn't have that…" He flashed a sinister and facetious smile as his baton made more circles.

"Oh warden….I'm not looking to offend anyone," sighed Clark as he rose out of the chair and followed the deputy out the door and down the corridor. After moving through two sets of locked doors that required prison guards to activate a loud buzzer to be opened, the deputy led Clark to the same conference room where he had witnessed the prisoner have a seizure several days before. The room was gray with poorly lit fluorescent lights and a sickening shade of off beige paint. It smelled of urine and the green and white checkerboard linoleum tiles were caked with decades of dirt, disappointment and misery. Waiting in silence for his subject to appear for their meeting gave Clark a claustrophobic malaise so strong that just imagining what years spent inside the prison must be like caused a slight shortness of breath. Even though his interview had gotten cut short with the seizure last visit, Clark still had barely enough information for a story from interviews with Ms. Della Russo. But something about the whole case bothered him and Clark was in desperate need of answers.

The chinking sound of handcuff chains could be heard over the shuffling of large feet. The floor shook with vibrations as Joseph MacDougal entered the room flanked by two guards and sat across the table from Clark. He looked surprisingly calm, and a faint smile could be detected under his beard.

"You just can't stay away can you," said MacDougal under his breath. "Give me a heads up if you are going to flash any triggers this time Mr. Westfield."

"Yeah, um…sorry about that," said Clark. "I had no idea you were epileptic…"

"I'm not!" MacDougal shot back. 'I've never been epileptic – EVER!"

"Well the warden said.."

"Of course, the warden said that. He is probably in on it too," growled MacDougal. "they all are!"

"In on what?" sighed Clark. Suddenly he wished he hadn't come back to complete the interview. No amount of journalistic due diligence was going to mitigate the unpleasantness of listening to the ravings of a cold-blooded lunatic who seemed to be losing his grip on reality. Clark sank down in his seat dejected and thought silently to himself he didn't find any aspect of his job fun anymore.

"Mr. Westfield, it's time you and I had a heart-to-heart talk," MacDougal hissed. Clark got out his reporter's notebook and mustered a contrived smile.

"I'm all ears Mr. MacDougal," Clark said dismissively. He suddenly wanted to be absolutely anywhere on earth other than seated in that chair in the room with Joseph MacDougal.

"I had a seizure last time you were here because you showed me my homing trigger. So, you are either working with them or you are about to uncover one of the biggest stories you've ever worked on." MacDougal eyes beamed maniacally as he spoke.

"Well, I'm not working with anyone – I'm not even sure if my editor likes me or if I'll have a job when I get back to the office, so what is this big scoop you are going to tell me about?" asked Clark intolerantly.

"I was one of their assassins. I signed up for free drugs. I never intended to kill anybody. I was just gonna shake it off and keep getting the free acid hits and they just kept dosing me. Then one day I wake up and there's blood on my basement floor and I realize they had gone ahead and succeeded in the control ops…and" MacDougal was talking so fast he was almost out of breath.

"Who is 'they'? What control ops and free drugs? What are you even talking about?" said Clark, clearly frustrated. "You know what –

one second," Clark took his digital tape recorder out of his pocket and put it on the table. "Mind if I get this on tape this time? Start at the beginning – pretend I know nothing about the case please.."

MacDougal smirked – "Sure…I'll start from the beginning." He looked straight into Clark's eyes, a stare so intense it looked right through him. "In 1967 I had just graduated high school and I fell in love with this gorgeous dark-haired girl – Sandy. I was an anxious mess because if I didn't get into college I was going to have to go into the service. It was a living hell back then and there was no one to talk to. You didn't know from one day to the next what was going to happen. Could I marry her? Was I going to be sent off to war? Would I make enough money? You have no idea what uncertainty can do to a young man. So, one day, Sandy takes me to Lake Sebago up in Harriman State park to one of the camp lodges around the lake and we sit in the dining hall with some other people and she asks me if I want to try a spiritual trip. I had nothing to lose so I ate a sugar cube that was soaked in LSD. That time and that sugar cube gave me the best experience of my life. I truly saw how everything was interconnected and how there is a harmony to the universe that we don't see. When it was over, I thought I was in love with her and couldn't wait to do it again."

"Look, I'd simply like to hear why you think you should be paroled. I'm not going to have room for a biography piece, Mr. MacDougal," interrupted Clark.

"You'll listen to what I have to say in its entirety," MacDougal shot back. "So, after that first magical trip, all I wanted to do was go back and trip again. As it turned out, there were some men who would lead these LSD ceremonies on an almost nightly basis. A lot of times they would talk to us while we were spacing out. I didn't care because everything they were giving us was free. Then they started taking us for walks up in the woods, and they kept leading us to the entrance to the mine."

"You mean the Bradley Mine in Harriman State Park?" asked Clark.

"Yes exactly," answered MacDougal. "They would drop us off in different parts of the park with a blindfold and challenge us to find it in the dark or when we were tripping. It seemed like a game at first, and I thought I had found a group of friends that liked dropping acid and playing hide and seek in the woods. But at the end of the summer, they asked if we wanted to keep participating in the tripping games but they then called it civil defense orienteering. I didn't care what they called it, I just knew I didn't have to search for or pay for drugs and that's all I cared about. So as time went on, they had us standing in lines like soldiers, practicing fighting maneuvers, etc. Then once, when I was really high, I remember thinking I saw the others in the group gather around one of the participants and stab him. It was awful. I got so freaked out I ran screaming out of the dining hall and into the water. I was terrified. Everyone came out and got me onto the beach and stood with me with me just telling me it was a bad trip. They were so relaxed afterwards I believed them because I figured if they had all gathered around and stabbed somebody to death, they wouldn't be so calm. There was no reason for it, and I'm sure they would have killed me next rather than just let me watch. So, I convinced myself it was a bad trip. But I also thought I'd had enough and after that I went back home to Westvale."

"Forgive me but what does this have to do with the murder of the Della Russo boy?" asked Clark. He was getting impatient.

"I got a two-year teaching degree at Bergen Community College, then got a job as a history teacher which kept me out of the draft. But I couldn't stop thinking about that bad trip and after about two or three years I went back up to Lake Sebago in Harriman. I looked around but found nothing. Then I walked up to the mine. I saw a brass marker embedded in the dirt at the entrance - the same as the marker you found and I had my first seizure, right there in the woods. I lay on the ground for a while and almost choked on all the fluid that kept pouring out of my mouth and nose. It was awful. That's when I knew."

"Knew what?" asked Clark.

"It's when I knew the stabbing, I'd witnessed years ago in the camp dining hall was real. Then the whole thing finally made sense. All those ritual style drug parties had all kinds of weird shit going on. It was like somebody turned on the lights. I remembered being shouted at. All these memories that I never had before suddenly appeared and they were as real as I am talking to you here now. Whatever these parties were, they had an agenda and type of training aura to them." MacDougal slowed down as he kept describing the drug parties. It occurred to Clark that what MacDougal was describing could easily have been one of the MK Ultra experiments.

"So, then what happened?" Clark asked.

"So, then I went to work as a teacher. I loved the job and things were quiet as I lived with my mom and tried to forget everything," explained the murderer.

"And what happened to this 'Sandy'?" Clark asked.

"I never saw her again. That is not until later…" Macdougal's eyes looked down and he got quiet.

"I hate to sound like a broken record, but about the death of the Della Russo boy."

"Yeah so one day I saw this young boy walking up my path to my door, he looked so happy..and I really was going to buy a magazine subscription…" MacDougal got really quiet. Clark checked to make sure the tape recorder was working. "And the next thing I know a man was letting me out of a car and walked me up to my door saying go inside and get some rest, we'll take care of everything. Later I woke up in my basement and all I know is I smelled that same distinct puke smell from the first time I had a seizure and I had foam all over my shirt which was soaked. One sleeve had blood on it, but it wasn't mine."

"So, you had raped and killed little Anthony Della Russo," Clark asked as directly as he could. "Are you saying you had an accomplice?"

"I NEVER raped anybody! But I did in fact murder that boy." MacDougal got quiet and stared at the floor. He was getting emotional. Clark wanted him to continue to explain the murder but was trying to be careful not to trigger another seizure or enrage his subject. He was after all, in a room alone with an agitated child murderer in a jail where the warden already resented him. "Yes. I killed him. I feel horrible about it. But it wasn't really me. During all those trip sessions there was some kind of thing they did with us, and they kept using shapes and shouting. And they kept showing us the mine and those medallions and saying to report to the mine when we are activated....report to the mine when you're activated..report to the mine when activated..."

Clark broke the silence. "So....you got activated and reported to the mine?"

MacDougal nodded as tears streamed down his face.

"And when you say activated," Clark made air quotes as he spoke. "You mean you raped and killed an innocent seven-year-old boy…" MacDougal raised his head and snarled at Clark: "I NEVER raped anybody. Whatever happened set it off – I don't know why. "

"You were charged with sexual assault – did that somehow magically happen on its own?" Clark had a hard time hiding his sarcasm as he thought of the drug fueled frenzy that must have occurred between this giant man and his tiny victim.

"I don't know – all I know is that I definitely didn't assault anyone. It's like a rage came out of nowhere. I had never met this boy before. I had no animosity towards him. Then all of a sudden, this wash of heat and anger came over me and the next thing I knew I was waking up in my basement and I vaguely remembered being dropped off. When the police came to my house, I knew I needed to take them to the mine, but I didn't know what would be up there. I figured if I didn't kill him then we wouldn't find anything and if I did kill him then I was accurate in my recollection…so we went up and there he was…and the only way I could have known that is if I killed him and put him there."

"So, you have no recollection of the actual killing?" asked Clark. His heart was in his throat, and he could hear his pulse. Suddenly the room felt very cold. MacDougal continued looking at the table.

"I remember letting him in, and then getting dropped off back at my house. That's it. For years afterwards I kept repeating to myself 'Upon activation report to the mine'. Sometimes I still say it. I don't know why. I don't know what happened." MacDougal said in almost a whisper.

"So let me get this straight…" Clark leaned in his chair and took a moment to try to strike as nonchalant and respectful a tone as possible. "You were an eager participant in long term powerful psychotropic drug use, some of which involved violent hallucinations. You remember answering the door as a young boy knocked on it. You have no recollection of harming him. But after he was missing for three days you had no trouble leading police to the body which was deliberately concealed in the woods at a very specific place that you visited several times while high and you deny you had anything to do with it?" Clark still sounded incredulous despite his attempts to tone it down.

"I'm not denying I had anything to do with it," said MacDougal, staring Clark down. "I'm saying I probably did but it's got something to do with those parties we used to have. But I never raped or sexually assaulted anybody. I don't know what happened – I just know there is a lot more to this whole thing and we could find out a lot more if we ever found the man who drove me home and if we could ever find Sandy."

"You never saw Sandy again?" asked Clark, unsure of what to make of everything he was hearing.

"I saw her one more time," MacDougal took a deep breath. "I saw her the day I entered my plea and was sentenced in court. She was seated right behind your dad in the courtroom. I don't know why she was there; I didn't get to say anything to her. "

"Ok..well why are you telling me this story now?" pressed Clark. "Why didn't you say this at your trial or at least one of your prior parole hearings? For Christ's sake you pleaded guilty Mr. MacDougal!"

"Your fucking father convinced me to plead no contest! It WASN'T a guilty plea. It was a no contest plea. Big difference.." shouted MacDougal.

"Well, not in the eyes of the law when it comes to sentencing," countered Clark.

"And I never plead guilty to any molestation or assault charges. They just got dismissed when they realized they had enough on the murder charge. Your father knew all this. He thought it would get me an even harsher sentence if I fought it, so I listened to him and entered the no contest plea." For a man capable of such nonsensical horror and the emotional incoherence it would take to murder a child, at that moment he sounded incredibly lucid and rational. Clark didn't know what to make of any of it and tried to picture his father attempting to talk sense and help a client who was far beyond any conceivable redemption.

"So, is anything you told me enough of a reason for you to be granted parole?" Clark challenged.

"No," said MacDougal coldly.

"No?" Clark retorted.

"No. Not even a little. If I blacked out and murdered someone then I'll always have that potential and I shouldn't be out in the world. And if I was in fact activated, then god forbid it happens again. No, I belong here Mr. Westfield. I've grown used to it." MacDougal said softly.

"So…if you don't want to be granted parole why are you telling me all this?" asked Clark, genuinely puzzled.

"Because…you're a smart man. Now you know what's up in that mine and you know there is a lot more to this story than people realize. Plus…now you want to know whether your dad knew..and if he did, why would he bury it all?" As MacDougal spoke Clark swallowed hard. He tried not to reveal through his expression that much of everything Joseph MacDougal had just told him had already been corroborated in his research. But it would be a tough sell for Clark to believe his father tampered with or hid any evidence. His worried look gave it away.

"You know this to be true don't you Mr. Westfield," said MacDougal grinning. "I'm not trying to get out of here. I like it here. I'm trying to get you to report the truth because you can't NOT report the truth. It's not in your nature. Even if it means exposing the reality that your father was in on whatever happened? Doesn't that explain the sad worried look I see on the face of the great Clark Westfield? That's Peabody Award winning investigative journalist and columnist CLARK WESTFIELD!??" MacDougal widened an evil grin. He had gotten deep inside Clark's head.

"Fuck you," Clark muttered and rose from the table and walked out of the room leaving the murderer there seated snickering and laughing.

"Find Sandy! Find the man who dropped me off! Those are your next clues Westfield! Thanks for doing all this for me!" MacDougal's voice trailed off as Clark hastened his pace down the prison corridor to the first buzzing lock towards the men's room. Bile surged in his stomach, and he could feel the pressure of a gag reflexing back the fluid into the back of his throat.

"Fuck you," Clark said aloud again and flung open the men's room door as he vomited all over the urinal and wished he had never turned over that box in the garage so many years ago…

Chapter 8

Clark stood on the front porch of the three-bedroom split level ranch on the end of the Cul De Sac in Westvale. He looked at the mailbox where the letter D in the family name DellaRusso had broken off the embroidered plastic and left a dark smudge outline on the tin. He told himself he would just collect his thoughts and try to lower his heart rate before ringing the doorbell, but the July heat filled his airways with a steamy, dirty, New Jersey heaviness that seemed to get more polluted the older he got. As he stood deep in thought, the wooden door opened and there stood an old woman on the other side of the screen. Isabella Della Russo's gaze shot through the tiny metal squares of the storm door mesh, and she said nothing.

"Oh, hello, Ms. Della Russo…I'm glad you're home.." stammered Clark. "I know I didn't call and arrange a meeting, but I thought if you had a moment…."

Isabella Della Russo pushed the latch on the door handle and opened the storm door.

"I knew you'd be back," said Ms. Della Russo coldly. "Please come in as you're letting my air conditioning cool the neighborhood."

Clark nodded and stepped inside the foyer and followed the elderly lady to the couch.

Clark sat down on the couch and they both stared at each other in silence. He wondered why Ms. Della Russo claimed to know he would return. But the dimly lit silence between them that hung in the air was so catastrophically uncomfortable that he figured he should get right to the point and not make this anymore awkward or painful than it needed to be.

"Ms. Della Russo…" Clark started speaking then paused. "I want you to know that I don't have an agenda of any kind, and I also want to make a commitment to you for total transparency. You deserve it after all you've endured and after indulging me in my interview requests. Let's also acknowledge that since my father was the defense attorney for the man who murdered your son, there is probably some understandable resentment or at the very least some discomfort between us. Since we last met I've done a series of interviews and additional research, including another interview with Joseph MacDougal in prison and I'm looking to corroborate.."

"Really Mr. Westfield?" Isabella Della Russo cut him off mid-sentence. "Are you really looking to corroborate your ace reporter research?"

"I'm sorry?" asked Clark, taken aback by her hostility.

"You don't need me to corroborate anything," shot Isabella Della Russo in a cutting tone. "I know why you are here. I know what you've heard or discovered or read or whatever you reporters do..and I know what you really want is absolution for the memory of your father because the story you are working doesn't have you horrified about my little boy Anthony and how he died in a pool of his own blood – it's really about whether your father buried evidence isn't it Mr. Westfield?"

Clark was aghast. He felt his stomach drop and the saliva drain from his mouth and throat. His heart rate quickened higher than any pace he felt before ringing the doorbell. "how..how do you know?" he stammered.

"Despite my contempt for both you and your father, I'll concede you are both pretty smart and I knew we'd be having this conversation eventually." Her voice trailed off and she sat waiting for Clark to speak. Clark swallowed hard. He found the strength to speak after several seconds.

"In the course of my research and interviews, I've come across evidence that might help explain why your son was murdered," Clark said slowly. "There is a real possibility that Joseph Macdougal was impaired by a domestic clandestine paramilitary program and that it had something to do with his violent tendencies and.."

"Let me spare you the soliloquy Mr. Westfield," Isabella Della Russo's teeth showed as she spoke, and her expression changed to seering anger. "You don't get to waltz in here and grandstand your skills of discovery like you solved some dinner theater murder mystery. So, you are here to take a victory lap in telling a murdered boy's grieving mother that there was more to the story and I could probably sue the government in civil court and it's all going to be ok. Meanwhile you'll get another journalism award to stroke your ego by publishing information that sways the parole board and lets the devil back out on the street to rape and murder another innocent child. I've heard it ALL before. Your father showed up here 25 years ago with the same story trying to unburden his conscience. I'll tell you what I told him then – I'm all for cooperating if it brings my son back. Until then, both Clark Westfield father and son can go fuck themselves." Her voice hadn't raised a notch but the passion in her tone was overwhelming.

"My dad came to see you? When?" Suddenly Clark no longer felt like a reporter with a deadline, but more like a son who missed his dad.

"After church one day," Isabella continued. "Your father was very bothered by the role of a certain Catholic priest, wasn't he?"

"I knew because Father Murphy came to see me in 1973 and said that your father had made a motion to get MacDougal's confession thrown out of court, claiming that because it was technically done during the sacrament of confession under the seal of the confessional it was legally protected and therefore inadmissible as evidence. That meant the police had no probable cause for arrest, which meant any evidence that came from that arrest – including the discovery of his body – would be inadmissible as evidence. The whole case was likely going to be thrown out," explained Ms. Dela Russo.

"Why did Father Murphy come tell you this? Why not the prosecutor's office?" asked Clark, perplexed.

"He showed up here one night and told me because your father had given him a black eye for disclosing evidence obtained under the seal of a priest/penitent confession," she continued. "But in addition to explaining his injuries he wanted me to know what a grave sin he had committed and that he was going to have to admit it in open court. Breaking the seal of the confessional was a Cardinal sin, technically only the Pope himself can forgive such an egregious breach of sanctified trust. Father Murphy kept saying he didn't expect me to forgive him and that he felt he owed me an explanation before it all started coming out in court."

"My dad gave him a black eye?" asked Clark somewhat bemused. "So, what did you say?"

"I threw him out and wished him the best of luck with his search for redemption because he certainly wasn't going to get any forgiveness from me. I then told him that it felt like he had murdered my son all over again. He left and he died a short time later." Clark thought a minute, completely thrown by what he was hearing.

"But…my father never filed that defense motion…" said Clark as he tried to stitch the puzzle together in his head.

"Obviously not. Next I heard was that he was going to plead guilty and there wouldn't be a long trial and I would have to speak at the sentencing – which I did and now thanks to the screwed up laws in this state and know-it-all heroes like yourself I still have to repeat myself every few years in front of the parole board," said Isabella Della Russo matter of factly.

"So…wait….why didn't my father mount that legal defense? Did anyone ever say anything? Something must have happened, and dad wouldn't have let that go - especially if it involved breaking the seal of confession and as such a devout Catholic…" Clark was starting to speak faster as he realized this was an additional reason his father would have never supported a guilty plea.

"As you know, your father was very involved in our church – that same church that you went to as a child and obviously no longer attend," her tone returned to its cutting nature. "One day, at least ten years after we lost my son, we were at a parish business meeting, and I found myself sitting next to your father – completely unplanned. I made an assumption that he probably wanted some kind of validation for not bringing the protected clergy communication in as a way to get the case thrown out and let him know that he actually saved many people massive amounts of pain – so I took him aside quietly and thanked him for never filing the motion and told him that I sent Father Murphy on his way that night with nothing but disgust."

"You talked to my dad about it? What did he say?" Clark felt a lump form in his throat knowing that he might be about to hear his father had committed legal malpractice.

"He said nothing. He simply looked at me, his eyes filled with tears, and he walked away," she said.

"So that's it?" asked Clark somewhat deflated.

"Oh, not at all. Another ten years went by and then it was time for that bastard's second parole opportunity. By then I had to form my nonprofit and hold rallies and all kinds of other frustrating garbage that would keep him behind bars – it had become the focal point of my life by then and it was so unnecessary. Then your father came to see me…"

"He came and found you at your house? Like he just showed up?" asked Clark on the edge of his seat.

"Yup…he showed up just like you did this afternoon – right on the doorstep. I knew he would show up someday, but what he had to say wasn't what I expected." Isabella Della Russo's voice slowed down. "Instead of discussing the tainted confessional, he showed up with a box of files, and explained that Joseph MacDougal had been unknowingly recruited into a government program that would train what he called passive operatives. In other words, this program manipulated people using drugs and other mind control techniques to do things like commit burglaries and assassinations so it couldn't be traced back to the government – and that MacDougal was one of the recruits when the training mechanism had somehow malfunctioned and killed my son. Your father said I had a clear case to sue in civil court and the federal government would almost certainly settle out of court to avoid embarrassment. I didn't know what shocked me more, the wild fantastic details of a CIA caper or that if this came to light your father would have been disbarred for burying the mitigating evidence. He said he would gladly face the music of the bar association and however they chose to penalize him if I went on the record about Father Murphy's botched confession and that a Catholic priest had screwed up so badly."

"Jesus…my dad was willing to get disbarred over the MK Ultra evidence?" asked Clark who was struggling to process what he was hearing. "So, what did you do?"

"I told him with Father Murphy dead there was no point in shaking the congregation's faith in the institution's leadership further – it would just prevent criminals from confessing in the future as well as the average person," she explained. "Then I told him that no amount of money in a government civil suit was going to bring my son back, and worse it may even get this guy released from prison where he could hurt someone again. And I just couldn't let that happen.."

"So, what did you do?" asked Clark

"Your father told me that the files were mine to do with what I wished and that if I chose to pursue it I would have his cooperation and honesty and assistance and he let." Isabella Della Russo paused and took a deep breath. "And as soon as your father's car pulled out of the Cul De Sac I went to the garage and got the gas can for the lawnmower, poured gasoline over the two boxes and threw a match on the files. Your father had a problem with a guilty conscience and wanted a bad priest to be shamed. I had a different problem. I have a dead son and I have to plead every few years that the man who sexually assaulted and killed him shouldn't be running loose. Once it was my decision, I had no problem deciding what to do."

"But Ms. Della Russo, with all due respect - there is a man in prison whose share of responsibility doesn't bear the sentence he has been given…that's not your judgment call to make." Clark gasped incredulously.

"Perhaps," said Isabella Della Russo thoughtfully. "But I'm a mother whose son was raped and murdered. I only have one set of criteria, which is: will it bring my son back? And if the answer is no then it's not my concern." She sat coldly staring at Clark who sat digesting all he had just heard.

"Joseph Mc Dougal says he didn't sexually assault your son. He says he most likely killed him but can't remember and he denies raping him. And in examining the guilty plea, he only pleaded no contest to manslaughter – he never entered a plea on the sexual assault charge, and it was thrown out…why was that?" asked Clark who seemed to suddenly hone in the emphasis MacDougal had put on denying the assault in his prison visit.

"The prosecutors told me he was giving them a hard time on the rape charge, and they said that while there were injuries, they didn't have any physical evidence from him – no body fluids, blood or sperm – and it was going to possibly hold everything up for years. So I told them to get him to plead to the murder charge and forget about it. And that's what they did and that's what put him where he belongs," said Isabell gritting her teeth. Clark sat with his mind racing. He sensed Ms. Della Russo's growing impatience and also realized this would likely be his last interview with her. He glanced at the classic boy scout portrait of young Anthony that stood in an 8x10 frame on the end table next to the sofa. It was the same classic portrait that was in the shrine at the church and that his paper had published each time they ran an incremental story.

"One last question Ms. Della Russo and then I will be going," said Clark as he pointed to the photo. "This patch on his uniform – the one that looks like a merit badge or something…what is that?"

"That? Oh, that's the merit badge he earned for learning and mastering Morse code. He loved it. Back in 1973 that was still used in airports and the military and overseas communications. He used to be up in her room all night beeping and tapping. It drove us crazy." Isabella's Della Russo's eyes filled with tears.

"Did you know that was the same logo as…"

"As some CIA project or trigger or something? Yes I knew….that was all in the files I burned. Frankly I don't care. And I'd like you to leave now," she said curtly. Clark got up from the sofa and walked over towards the door, sweat streaming down his face.

"Mr. Westfield - At the end of the day your father was a good man and did the right thing," said Isabella Della Russo in a cold monotone voice. "It will be interesting to read your piece and see if you are anything like him.."

And just like that, the door shut behind Clark and he was left in the silence of the dirty July New Jersey heat…

✳✳✳

✳✳✳✳✳✳✳✳

Elizabeth Cranford let the cardboard box land on her new desk with a thud. It was full of picture frames containing family photos of her parents and college roommates. Several contained journalisms awards she had won over the years. Two heavy ornate sculptures had a large crystal pyramid engraved with "New Jersey Press Association Award for Community Reporting Excellence 2015 Elizabeth Cranford" and 2014 on the other. These two journalism accolades were a personal and professional highlight for Elizabeth, unmatched in exuberance and satisfaction that is, until she was able place them down on her new heavy oak desk in a new office with a door that had "City Editor" on a brass plate. She walked around to the desk chair and sat down. On her right was a glass wall that looked out on the massive newsroom and all the reporters, assistants and interns feverishly typing on their computers and hunched over tablets. On her left was a floor to ceiling window that looked over the skyline of Newark NJ. A thick brown smudgy mist hung over the city just above the roof of the Broad National Bank building on the corner of Broad and Market streets. Adjacent to the old Kreske department store skyscraper, it had been converted into college dormitories for Rutgers University. She drew in a deep breath. She had arrived – and it felt good. What felt even better was only she knew the depth of the story that Clark Westfield, Richie Byrne and herself were working on and the national impact it would make when it was revealed the strange local connection of unethical Cold War era intelligence measures and the link local New Jersey murder. It was almost too good to be true - her first major, Sunday edition-leading piece as the new City Editor would be a bombshell revelation and history challenging expose. She heard a tap on the glass. Sean Caldwell was standing at the wall window with a small flat brass name plate pressed against the window with her name on it.

"Ta da!" sang Sean Caldwell as he stepped into the doorway and began wiggling it into the grooved slot beneath the City Editor plate. "Elizabeth Cranford – City Editor! I can't tell you how happy this makes me!" Caldwell sounded genuinely pleased. "Hey, we have to go out for a drink tonight and celebrate, ok? Can I buy you an editor's shot tonight?" he said boyishly.

"Editor's shot? There is such a thing?" asked Elizabeth playfully. Despite her secretly loathing Sean Caldwell, the fact was that he had promoted her, and she saw it as bad karma to diminish any due gratitude. "Yes, I think a drink is in order later as it's been a long road getting here," she said with a sigh. It was then she noticed a man standing to Caldwell's left that she didn't recognize. The man stood there expressionless, peering through the glass at Elizabeth. He was old – possibly late 70's and was dressed in a black suit white dress shirt and black tie – rather formal for July heat in 2016. He had round glasses with shaded lenses and a sloppy mustache. In his left hand he held a square black briefcase. Caldwell sensed Elizabeth's perplexed look and realized an introduction was in order.

"Oh…I'm sorry! – Liz, this is William Bromley – may we come in for a moment?" Caldwell strode to the front of Elizabeth's desk and beckoned for this new stranger to come into the office as he sat down in one of the chairs opposite Elizabeth's desk. The mysterious Mr. Bromley glided in and sat in the other chair, staring at Elizabeth still expressionless. "Mr. Bromley is with the new owners, he stopped by today to see some of the new reorganization which includes your new post and he specifically asked to meet you," said Caldwell with his usual smug smile under his voice. Turning to Bromley, Caldwell said "Well, here she is, at her new desk in her new position of control – proud and well deserved – I present to you Ms. Elizabeth Cranford, my finest protégé" Bromley continued his fixed gaze on her but said nothing.

"Well, it's nice to meet you Mr. Bromley," said Elizabeth. "Thank you both for coming by in a welcome wagon visit on my first day – as you can see, I'm still unpacking. It's really nice to have an office with a door - who knew privacy carried such prestige?" said Elizabeth, smiling and attempting to break the ice. "What exactly do you do with the new owner group?"

Bromley continued to stare at her as if she hadn't spoken at all and Caldwell broke the awkward silence.

"Liz, not to put you on the spot or anything but I told William here that you'd give us a preview of some of your upcoming tentpole pieces that you've been working on. I talked you up quite a bit but I'm sure he would like to hear it from you if you have a minute. What do you have on the grid there, Liz?" Elizabeth felt a hot swell of anger at Caldwell for putting her on the spot in front of a stranger from the owner company in her first few minutes as new city editor. But then she realized that assuming the editor's chair meant signing up for unexpected pop quizzes and thinking quickly on her feet. She swallowed to clear any anxiety from her voice and tried to muster a smile.

"Well…," Elizabeth allowed a pause to create anticipation. "We've got a long-term investigation into sex abuse by clergy in the Newark Archdiocese that involves pouring over years of internal church personnel records. That is going to take some time and once we have our database the plan is to conduct thorough interviews with victims, families and fellow clergy so we are aiming for a big fourth quarter series.."

"Well, that's down the road a bit…what's your big opening piece? Tell us about that," interrupted Caldwell, sounding slightly anxious Elizabeth wasn't talking about next week's stories.

"Oh well, next week we are planning a big series on the upcoming parole hearing for child murderer Joseph MacDougal – the case has been a major blockbuster here in NJ for more than 40 years and each time he comes up for parole there are new angles and new interviews. He probably won't get parole of course, but it's always an opportunity to examine the evolution of criminal law and other aspects of the case." Elizabeth felt a cold tension in the air as this new visitor continued to simply look at her and say nothing. She sensed she should hold back on the details but didn't exactly know why.

"Yeah, Will, it's gonna be great," interjected Caldwell. "They've got interviews with the murderer and the victim's mother – we sent someone to find the police team that worked the original crime, we've got expert legal analysis because there has been a law passed since the crime happened – this is our story and we've been on it literally since the boy disappeared back in 1973.."

"Well, I have to say the guy that deserves credit is Clark Westfield – he has been on this story his whole life." Elizabeth cut Caldwell off and wasn't going to allow him to bury Clark's lifelong reporting work on the case. "In fact, it's the first story he published here back when he started and when I started as his intern after reading..."

"Where is Mr. Westfield today?" asked William Bromley abruptly without breaking his intense stare in the slightest. His sudden question took them both by surprise as it was the first words he had spoken.

"Clark? Oh well, Clark is usually out working on interviews and he does some writing at home – you know these old guys – he is probably….uh Liz, is Clark here today?" asked Caldwell nervously glancing over the newsroom.

"Clark is out on assignment right now. Why do you ask?" Elizabeth sensed something was up and she wanted to know what.

"Westfield now reports to you right?" asked Bromley directly.

"Well, I guess technically, yes – but having worked under him for so long after he hired me out of college, I don't think he needs my oversight in the way the rest of the department does." Elizabeth was slightly baffled by this mysterious newcomer's interest in Clark. Without breaking his gaze from Elizabeth's, Bromley quietly directed a question at Caldwell.

"Sean, can you give Ms. Cranford and I a moment together?" he asked coldly.

"Sure – ask her anything you want. I made her city editor for a reason and she has always delivered when.."

"I mean leave us alone and shut the door behind you," said Bromley, still keeping his gaze on Elizabeth, barely blinking.

"Oh…umm…ok sure…. I'll, uh, just be in my office and let you two get to know one another," Caldwell stammered and got out of his chair with a perplexed look on his face. As he stepped immediately behind William Bromley he gave Elizabeth the OK sign with his hand in an attempt at a corny reassurance. The door shut behind him and he stood in the hallway pretending to talk to staff while still peering in the window. After several seconds of silence Bromley spoke.

"You think he is a condescending prick, don't you?" he asked Elizabeth in his low robotic voice. Quite taken aback by the nature of the question, she immediately realized this was a guest with an agenda. Until she knew what that might be, agreeing with a disparaging statement about her superior seemed like an obviously bad idea.

"I'm sorry?" she asked, trying to seem as nonchalant and quizzical as possible.

"It's ok, I'm not asking for you to confirm my observations," Bromley replied. "I'd like to know more about your series next week on the upcoming parole hearing. The new owners are very excited that you've been selected for the city editor position, and we'd like to know how we can support you, so can you give me a verbal outline of what you plan to publish?" His expressionless face chilled Elizabeth slightly. Clearly this man whom she had never met, had both the authority and audacity to send her superior out of the room and demand an audit of her work. Maybe this was par for the course in editor accountability, but something didn't feel right.

"I'd be happy to," Elizabeth said kindly. "But before we dive into the details can you tell me a little bit about the new owner group as I'm clearly new to the position and I haven't gotten a chance to get up to speed on the managerial 'who's who' if you catch my drift." There was a pause filled with silence. "Mr. Bromley, with all due respect I would like to know who I'm talking to – that's fair isn't it?" Elizabeth felt the volume of her voice drop and her intimidation swell.

"You seem like a bright woman Ms. Cranford, and you didn't become editor without knowing how to placate men like Sean Caldwell and Clark Westfield while sidestepping a few landmines, so I'll just cut to the chase rather than insult your intelligence," said Bromley, as steady as before. "I represent a collective of concerned parties. We are in fact the owners of this newspaper among other media outlets and various businesses. We stand to benefit financially when you do your job well as you have been doing all this time. We will of course reward you as you continue to do so. However, we also stand to lose money and other conveniences with the various ripple effects of irresponsible reporting. So, when we spot an iceberg in the distance that represents a financial or repetitional risk due to say… unsubstantiated theories or information gathered while trespassing or national security breaches that would leave us open to litigation…or god forbid charges, we feel well within our purview to intervene. And among the owners and the board, your upcoming series about this parole hearing has everyone concerned – especially given Mr. Westfield's – shall we say 'preoccupation' with the far-fetched and wild world of conspiracy reporting."

"I haven't turned in a draft of the story yet – I haven't even given Sean an outline because we are still working on it so I'm perplexed as to what specifically could be concerning you," said Elizabeth rather curtly. While the visit from the corporate top brass was intimidating and anxiety inducing, it quickly gave way to visceral anger at the possibility management was monitoring reporter's information gathering, and the implication of justified news interference. Elizabeth hadn't spent her career putting in the blood, sweat and humiliation only to become editor and be told what was or wasn't news and grant favors.

"Well let's just say it's not in the interest of the owners or frankly this newspaper to indulge in anything other than a cursory report on the outcome of the parole hearing, and I suggest you assign one of the graduate fellows to cover the story. Mr. Westfield's talents are best used elsewhere in the time he has left – perhaps a survey of roadside cuisine around the Garden State would be attractive to advertisers, yes?" Bromley's expression changed slightly into a patronizing grin. Elizabeth was fuming inside but knew she needed to keep her cool and think clearly.

"Mr. Bromley – I don't operate in hypotheticals. And I understand that you and your investors – whomever they may be – would be naturally concerned about me coming on as a new editor, especially being a young African American woman from the projects in Newark and not understanding – how did you put it…'big business concerns and icebergs' and all. But Clark Westfield's journalism skills aren't up for subjective debate between the likes of you and I. It's already been decided by the panel judges at the Pulitzer, Peabody and Edward R. Murrow awards ceremonies. Over several decades they have thankfully objectively validated his skills which we are unable to do as mere mortals. As for my ability to determine news value and authenticity – I'd like to think I've done something right over the years or my name wouldn't be on the door under the title city editor. And as for your associates and their financial concerns, I suggest if they are worried that news published by this paper would hurt them financially or reputationally then maybe the newspaper business isn't the right place for them. Maybe they would feel better investing in something less confrontational with less ethics. A business such as shall we say – roadside cuisine?" Elizabeth was equally cool in her delivery. Bromley's expression changed into a slight smile that seemed to indicate he appreciated dealing with a worthy adversary.

"Well played Ms. Cranford," he said slowly. "Let me make this perfectly clear, though, while the option for you to do the right thing remains on the table..." Bromley paused and let the silence highlight the importance of what he was about to say. "We both know this has nothing to do with you being a black woman. I assumed you were smart enough to know that if someone calls your bluff when you place the race and gender card it usually blows up in your face. But that's neither here nor there and you'll learn that eventually. You trespassed on government property, which is on record. You compromised classified government sources and files which are also on the record. After you wreak havoc with your upcoming series written by your delusional superstar reporter, the only result is that a monster who raped and murdered a seven-year-old may get to walk free. And well, we simply can't have that. So, I am telling you, nicely, as a new friend, that the MacDougal series doesn't see the light of day. It would be nice if you had this editorial position for a long time and didn't prove unreliable on your first day. I've saved you the embarrassment of telling you this in front of your boss – who frankly, no one has much respect for. We've got big plans for you Elizabeth, even a nice little black girl from Newark like you."

Elizabeth was thunderstruck. How did Mr. Bromley know about their trip to the mine, discovery of the bunker and interviews in Washington? Further, who were these shadowy new "owners" that stood to lose financially if Clark's series was published. Elizabeth had worked her entire life to get into the chair in which she was now seated, and within 15 minutes of sitting down she was being strong armed in a story and her job was being threatened. She swallowed hard.

"So… what am I supposed to tell Caldwell…and Clark?" she asked in a meek voice.

"We'll handle Caldwell, and you won't get any heat. He doesn't need to know any of the details of what you've collected so far – leave him to us. As for Westfield, well, you are his editor, aren't you? He works for you…" Bromley said as he Isabella from his chair. As he stepped back towards the door, he turned to face Elizabeth one last time. "Just carry on and go forward like none of this ever happened…..and you'll be fine." And just like that, William Bromley turned and opened the door and left. Sean Caldwell was twenty feet outside watching the door and immediately hurried over to Bromley who continued to walk down the hallway right past him. Caldwell doubled back and leaned into Elizabeth's office.

"All good? Nice guy, right? What did you guys talk about?" he asked nervously.

"Roadside cuisine.." replied Elizabeth quietly gazing out the window in the distance.

Elizabeth sat in her car in the parking garage and exhaled. The blank cement wall in front of her car's hood was a perfect metaphor for the recent meeting. After the exchange in her office with the odd Mr. Bromley she needed time to decompress. Normally, when an older white man told her she couldn't do something she simply tried harder and ensured it got done. Elizabeth had never worried about rules, guidelines or even laws when she knew what she was doing was right. But something about this scared her. Whomever this mysterious Mr. Bromley was, he knew about all the research activity that she and Clark had conducted in the field. Deep in the pit of her stomach she felt like the ethics of being a newspaper editor and the judgment and discretion she was trusted to wield over story content didn't apply here. She also realized that with Bromley excluding her immediate superior from the equation, she had no internal professional recourse without Sean Caldwell. As she reflected on her nerve-racking predicament, she told herself that maybe there was a grand payoff if she played ball. Maybe there was a bigger picture of which she simply was not yet aware. She didn't believe that, but thinking it over at least let her heart rate return to a normal pace. She kept hearing his smug old man's hoarse larynx cords say "A nice little black girl like you…" Her temperature rose as she stared at the wall drawing deep breaths. Suddenly she heard a whimper. Looking around in the dimly lit parking deck she saw Richie Byrne's car on her left. He was seated in the driver's seat with both hands in the 12 o'clock position and his head resting against the backs of his wrists. His shoulders were shaking. He was crying rhythmically. Elizabeth got out of her car and walked around to the driver's side window of Richie's car.

"Hey..," she tapped gently on the window. "Hey…Byrne..you ok?" Richie woke with a start and looked like he had been thrown in an icy bathtub. When he saw it was Elizabeth he exhaled in relief. He rolled down the window.

"Hey Liz…I'm glad it's you. Get in – we gotta talk." Richie sounded out of breath as he spoke.

"Are you ok? Why are you sitting out here in the garage on your own sobbing?" Elizabeth cracked a smile when she spoke trying to break the tension and let him know she was concerned.

"It's bad Liz…" Richie sighed and stared straight ahead at the concrete barriers.

"What's bad?" she asked.

"I came home and Melissa was crying." Richie stopped to choke back a sob. "They mailed her pictures…."

"Pictures of what?"

"Pictures of me and Kelly," tears streamed down Richie's face.

"Kelly as in….your Pentagon source?" Elizabeth asked quizzically.

"Yes. Kelly as in Lt. Colonel Kelly Pram," said Richie, his voice raising with frustration. "And pictures as in pictures of me and Kelly in bed." His eyes closed with embarrassment as he gave the sordid detail.

"Wait….I thought you and Kelly were done," asked Elizabeth.

"We were. Then I saw her again on our story trip and I was needing more details and one thing led to another and well…" Richie stopped, assuming she could imply what happened next. "So, I got home and somebody tailed us, shot pictures and got them to my wife. Right there in black and white in a manila envelope – like old school spy spook stuff. You'd think it would be easier to text her or email her – but they actually sent prints, probably so I couldn't do any computer forensics…"

"Did Melissa hire someone to follow you? Who would be onto you and why would they do that?" Elizabeth's tone then turned serious. "What were you working on with Kelly? What was she finding for you?"

"Umm.. well we were looking up enrollment records for CIA citizen recruitment for the Harriman Mine COG bunker story…"

"She was giving you records and names!?" Elizabeth exclaimed.

"Yeah, she always looked stuff up for me…look don't think I'm a bad person about the affair. It's really complicated, and it doesn't mean I don't love my wife."

"Richie – I couldn't care less about what you were doing or who with – but I gotta know – did she give you anything useful?" Elizabeth was now visibly nervous.

"Yeah – she confirmed that MacDougal was a recruit and has documentation on the Harriman Park recruitment site. Maps. Everything. But then she added a screen shot picture of a section of a document that said, "Staged sexual assault for child predator narrative" and I didn't know what that meant. "

"Well, have you asked her? And have you told her about the photos?" Asked Elizabeth.

"I called her – early this morning. She hasn't called or texted – I don't know if she is mad at something or me…I guess she should be…" Richie sighed again.

"Richie - she isn't mad at you," Elizabeth said slowly. "It's nothing like that."

"What do you think it is, Liz?" Richie asked her, tilting his head to one side.

Elizabeth spoke slowly in a whisper. "It means we are in over our heads…way over…"

Chapter 9

The hum of the old and dented window unit air conditioner rose above the oppressive heavy summer humidity, stirring along with the passive background noise New Jersey residents have grown so accustomed to as to be indistinguishable. Clark stood on the cement patio of the home of Stephen Miller, the editor who had mentored him as a young reporter and stood behind him during dozens of legal challenges, smear campaigns, advertiser threats and condemnation by public officials. If there was ever a time that Clark needed his guidance it was now, whether he was still editor or not. He pressed the doorbell that was smeared with white paint from the trim, then heard a voice from behind as Steve had come around the side of the house and up behind him.

"Westfield! What a nice surprise," said Miller with a smile. He was an older man with completely white hair and dressed as if he had been painting something. "What brings out the old dog warrior in this

July heat – you in trouble again?" The ancient editor's voice was hoarse from years of barking orders on midnight deadlines.

"Great to see some friendly fire, Steve," said Clark. His tone was heavy and dejected. Miller motioned for him to walk with him around the side of the house.

"I need to pick some of my tomatoes that I've been growing. You came at the perfect time!" he said as Clark wished they could go inside and out of the oppressive heat.

"Steve – can we sit inside its so fucking hot?" Clark asked practically gasping.

"Nah – it's not much cooler inside. I've been holding out on getting central air – when I moved in here 45 years ago there was only possibly about four weeks of the summer that you needed air conditioning if at all. Now you need it full blast right through the end of October! We are doomed I tell ya!" said Steve Miller with a laugh. "How have you been? What brings you out here? Though, it's really nice to just see you."

"Well, I need some advice from someone I respect," Clark said. "I'm on the MacDougal parole story and it's taken a few turns I need to discuss with you. First, because you are the guy that was on the job from the day of the murder right through his most recent parole hearing several years ago, you know the most about the case. And second, because that fucktard Caldwell doesn't know his head from ass and can't make a strategic decision if his life depended on it." His frustration was clearly evident.

"I always knew this day would come," said Steve Miller softly as he fondled his tomato plants. Clark looked perplexed as he heard the remark. "You were always an excellent reporter, Westfield. I always knew your curiosity was going to take you to places that were very confusing. What happened?"

"Oh, well, MacDougal is up for parole again," Miller nodded as Clark spoke. "And I've turned up a lot of details that I'm trying to make sense of. I finally went up to the mine where he hid the Della Russo boy's body —at his deranged suggestion. Turns out it's an old COG bunker that looks like it could still be operational if needed and when I showed him one of the markers, he had a full-blown seizure. You're not gonna believe this next part, but I had Richie Byrne work some of his Pentagon sources. Long story short, it looks like he was connected to some of the CIA training programs – likely one of the MK Ultra sub-projects. Then, I went back to the jail and interviewed him at length, and he said as much. It looks like Ms. Della Russo knew and…" Clark paused as he found the words to say next. "It looks like my father may have also known. So I need to ask you Steve…" Miller cut him off before he could ask his question.

"Before you ask me anything, I need to ask you a few things," said Miller. Something about his demeanor indicated to Clark he had been long prepared for the conversation they were having. "Is the world better off with MacDougal in or out of jail?"

"That's not the issue Steve, the issue is whether all these extenuating facts I've gathered are in some way exculpatory and whether the government had a hand in this tragedy, and frankly, whether my father knew…," said Clark. He was a bit surprised at Miller's question. "I didn't expect you – of all people – to hit me with whether the end justifies the means here…" The conversation had taken a surprising turn.

"Listen Clark – you of all people know how complicated details can get just under the surface. I trained you to go out and deconstruct all that in an effort to hold the world accountable. But the MacDougal case is different. He murdered and raped a seven-year-old boy. He pleaded guilty at your father's encouragement. What else is there really? Does it matter why?"

"He pleaded no contest, and he says he didn't rape him," Clark shot back defiantly.

"And you believe him? I'm a little surprised that you of all people would get manipulated by a child murderer but then they are a special breed…" said Miller.

"Steve – I'm not being manipulated. I've corroborated everything he has told me, and he doesn't even know it. But when it comes to manipulation, it's only you and I standing here, and you are the only person on the planet other than MacDougal who knows what happened decades ago when I didn't really get that first interview. You ran it like we had some big exclusive and you knew I had used the false attorney letter with my father's name to get into the prison and you still ran it and we've both lived with that all these years. So, when it comes to manipulation, I thought you'd at least have a perspective…" Clark was frustrated and his voice was rising. Steve Miller cut him off mid-sentence.

"Exactly! We both lived with it!" he exclaimed loudly but smiling. "And I think it worked out pretty well for us, Westfield – especially you! I NEVER printed anything that was actually untrue. I simply left out your fraudulent logistics because I saw the elements of an extraordinary reporter in there. When you fudged that letter all those years ago you were a wide eyed 22-year-old kid that was going to save the world with the energy of a lion. And when you had the sack to show up at that prison and get in that room, it meant you would do anything to get the job done and anything to get the story, even if it meant jeopardizing your career and your father's name. Anyone who is a true journalist and going to go the distance must have it in their nature to risk jail, death and sell their father's good name for a story – and there you were in my newsroom! So, I simply enabled you to do more of it and grow into the legendary Clark Westfield. Meanwhile, a child murderer is safely in prison, and you've written about the case beautifully over the years. Even a guy like you can't find a grievance in that equation!" Miller was still smiling. "So, I ask you again – is the world better and safer with MacDougal in prison or out?"

Clark was taken aback. He thought his old editor would be fascinated by the new details he had uncovered and would help sort through next steps including how to put together a story revealing the role any government programs had played leading up to the crime. But instead, he was encountering push back and an odd justification for keeping Joseph MacDougal in prison.

"You ran my first story all the years ago because you thought it would play well and keep this guy behind bars?" asked Clark in a low, meek voice.

"I ran your first story years ago because that is what the world needed to hear to make sense of the murder of a seven-year-old boy, Clark." Steve Miller's tone was suddenly serious. "I knew you technically violated the law in getting the interview and I knew you had nothing. So, I put my career and newspaper's reputation on the line because you had the one piece in this puzzle that was able to tie up the package for the general public. It's messy on the inside, but it's a neatly packaged win-win for everyone in every direction. Do you have any idea the reaction and panic it would create if the general public knew about some of these ties that you have finally found out about? Let me paint a picture for you: it would mean our own government had created an unknown group of terrifying and dangerous individuals that lived and worked among us in plain sight. Worst of all, it might mean this scumbag actually has a defense that could warrant his release from prison, and well, we just can't have that." Clark was shocked at what he was hearing. This was a man whose judgment he had never questioned in all the years he had known him, but he was now presenting himself as unrecognizable. Clark stammered to find the words.

"So, you've always known this?" Clark paused. "And you never said anything?" He was somewhat dumbfounded.

"Westfield…here is what I know," replied Steve Miller. "Part of my job as editor was exercising discretion when it came to details on all kinds of stories. Just because we find something when we are pursuing a story doesn't mean it needs to go in the paper because it could disrupt various efforts in place to keep us all safe. At the very least it simply might not be in the public interest. The good newspaper editors were the ones that understood man's brutal nature, need for dominance, capacity for irrationality, desire for vengeance, and his individual and collective ability to rationalize the horrors of racism, war and poverty. When one understands these truths, you also realize that metering certain information for the population through uniform education and daily news can often be the last filter between a healthy functioning society and total chaos. It's a matter of the greater good." Miller's smile was almost smug.

"The fucking Greater Good???!!!" Clark exclaimed. "What the hell are you talking about? Christ what happened to you, Steve? You were always the guy telling me to dig deeper – follow the money – question everything – find the agenda! For god sakes your motivational editor speeches read like a goddam comic book and now you admit you helped bury details for some fucked up greater good when we have a 7 year old boy dead? He was selling magazine subscriptions, Steve! He was fucking seven and he was a boy scout.."

"And he knocked on the wrong door and SHIT HAPPENED!" interrupted his old editor. Clark stood mouth agape. "Im as sad and angry as anybody about that tragedy but I had to make a judgment call years ago whether or not all those additional elements that you have so expertly now discovered were going to help or hurt the community that I served – that you served – that we all served – the community that a newspaper cultivates and cares for like a backyard tomato garden. It will thrive if you just give it the right care."

"The right care?" Clark gasped. "Do you even hear yourself right now?"

"Look – I don't know what you've found, and I don't want to know," said Miller, his old nurturing tone returning. "I do remember some of these coming up around the time of the original murder in discussions with your father, long before you graduated and faked your press access when you came to work for me. But it doesn't matter. What matters is that you understand the bigger picture. There is a greater good to be served here and I suggest that you seriously reflect on what impact and consequences your story would have if you published everything you've found so far. I'm sure there are really interesting elements in there. But what did you learn on countless police beats and other crime stories? You earn and groom sources more by what you don't report and who you protect than what you do put in the paper. Then, when something is really problematic, you are in a position to take action. That's the real power in a newspaper, Clark. That's how journalism remains a check and a balance on everything – the government, corporations, celebrities, pop culture – they all will keep answering to us as long as we are the ones who know how to keep the status quo. That's the real job of an editor."

"I feel like I don't know you anymore Steve, and frankly this is hard for me to hear," said Clark as Steve Miller picked another tomato. "So, you have no advice for me other than your bullshit cop out of don't rock the boat?"

"That's not at all what I'm saying. I'm simply saying you should ask yourself what have you got to prove? You are going to rewrite the history of murder case from 1973 and the only result is you might actually let the confessed murderer go free? You're smarter than that Clark. Plus – it doesn't matter. I don't know what you've found, and I don't care frankly. If you've truly found anything that is material and does in fact tie into counterintelligence efforts, then they will find you and it will be between you and them. Don't be afraid when that happens. It can be a more productive relationship than you think, and you'll realize soon enough we are all in this together."

"Who will find me? What are you talking about? Steve – seriously what the fuck?" Clark wondered for a moment if his old editor was in early dementia or cognitive decline.

"We're all in this together, Westfield – this experiment we call America. It's a beautiful idea with a beautiful story in it, but under the surface the details are messy. There is massive inequality and injustice, and people do bad things. But the myth survives because reporters like you and editors like me know what stories to tell. If we keep delivering that narrative to everyone's driveways every morning, neatly folded in black and white, it keeps us all on the same page literally and figuratively. No one knows this better than the people in charge in Washington. Sometimes we don't always know the role we play in all this. You've always been one of the best Clark, dammit you were the best I'd ever seen. I thought once I'd left, they would have reached out to you already but you hadn't written on anything too consequential since you abandoned that opioid story. God knows they don't trust Caldwell. But that's another story. They will find you once you get too close. Here is my advice – listen to them, hear them out, don't be a hero and try to see the bigger picture." Steve Miller extended his hand and grabbed Clark's as he finished speaking and shook it affectionately to indicate the discussion was over, turned towards his house with a basket of tomatoes he had picked hooked into the crook of his elbow, and walked towards his house leaving Clark standing in the hot backyard.

And just like that, Clark Westfield realized he was on his own.

****

****

As Elizabeth Cranford looked out the wall length window of her new city editor office at the Newark skyline, she felt sick to her stomach. She had worked her entire life to be able to stand and look out at the skyline of the city for which she was editor. Yet, she wasn't on the job a day before she faced enormous and ambiguous pressure from a shady owner's group who told her in no uncertain terms not to publish the upcoming story on Joseph MacDougal's parole hearing. But worse than the overt pressure and strong arming that she encountered in her new position, combined with the dismissive racism and disrespect the mysterious Mr. Bromley had shown her on behalf of the owner's group was that the story she was being asked to kill was Clark's. She could either stand up or fold when faced down with power – but screwing over her friend and mentor was going to be excruciating. What was she going to tell Clark?

A light knock sounded on the door and a dejected and sad Clark Westfield shuffled into the room with a heavy gait.

"Your name looks great on the door! This is the first time I'm seeing it," said Clark quietly. "For the record- I knew you were going to be great when I hired you, Liz." He managed a weak smile.

"Thank you. Where have you been? Never mind. Don't answer that. Clark, we have to talk," said Elizabeth taking a seat at her desk.

"I went to see our old boss, Steve Miller. I was on a quest for sanity. Have you seen Richie around?" Clark glanced through the wall window that looked out over the newsroom.

"You saw Steve? Oh my gosh – I was just thinking of him. How is he? God…I wish he were still here as we've got some complications, I've got to talk to you about. Wow – I wish I could get his advice right about now." Elizabeth said as she drew a deep breath.

"I'm not sure he would be of much help…" Clark said softly.

"What do you mean? What did he say? You know what…I need to tell you about something that happened while you were gone."

"Well, Steve sent his regards," Clark butted in. "You know you think you know somebody but then one day they just do something surprising and shocking…I went to Steve for advice on this story. A few things have come up. I needed his old school encouragement as well as editorial wisdom to help me navigate. I figured he was the one guy that could understand all this and knew all the players."

"Was he helpful? Because God knows we are going to need it," asked Elizabeth.

Clark sighed. "No. He gave me some fucked up reductionist pep talk about the greater good. No Liz, we are on our own. I've got a lot to tell you."

"I've got a lot to tell you," said Elizabeth. "Why don't you go first?"

"Well, Richie and I went down to Washington." As Clark spoke Elizabeth nodded. "And long story short we found out that the whole Harriman State Park was essentially set up as a recruitment and training proving ground for the military, and the CIA conducted elaborate operations there including various MK Ultra programs." Elizabeth's expression sank as Clark continued talking. "I went back to Trenton State Prison to interview MacDougal and he basically admitted to the murder of Anthony Della Russo, denied the sex assault, and said it was because some girlfriend of his at the time named Sandy brought him to camp meetings where they provided everyone with LSD and crazy rituals. Then years later in 1973 he woke up to police at his door and knew he had been what he described as 'activated,' and wound up under arrest for the murder. He says he has no recollection of the murder but it's likely that he did do it and he is vehemently denying the rape."

"And you believe him?" asked Elizabeth somewhat crossly. "Clark they all say that – have you ever met a murderer, especially one that is up for parole soon who says they remembered the details of their crimes?" Elizabeth had a thought that if she poked holes in his story enough maybe she wouldn't have to tell Clark about the flaming pressure that had found its way into her office earlier. But then, that would mean she was manipulating her old boss and he simply deserved better from her.

"I think Richie has a way to prove it. That's why I need to know where he is. He…found…some access to some of the MK Ultra recruitment files through his Pentagon contacts and I'm waiting for him to call – he isn't answering calls or texts which isn't like him. So, then I went to see Isabella Della Russo. And she was very curt with me and had no interest in any of the information from my prison interview but did tell me that father showed up many years ago with the same story and some files." Clark paused as he started to think about the complicated role his father had played in all this and how his upcoming story could very well cast a shadow on his father's handling of the case. "But all this is really important Liz, and if we need to get it in the paper before the hearing – this has potentially explosive implications and.."

"And you think you're going to get a convicted child murderer out of prison because the CIA did bad things 50 years ago?" Elizabeth challenged Clark. "Furthermore, I know I'm new to this editor job but I'm not exactly hearing the slow golf clap from the community we serve when this guy gets to go home."

"Jesus, Liz – who's side are you on?" shot Clark, suddenly riled. "I'm not trying to get anyone out of prison but there are facts in this case that a defendant is entitled to when making a case for parole. Plus, he has spent a lot of time in prison. But more importantly we may have evidence of a vast, deliberate, orchestrated CIA operation that happened right here in our backyard that was unethical, illegal and traumatic and ultimately resulted in the death of this little boy. If that's your first big tentpole story as city editor, then why am I not hearing a thank you? You were up in that mine with us! You know we are on to something big here."

"Yeah, maybe a little too big," said Elizabeth. "Clark, I had a visit from one of the owners."

"Did he come by to congratulate you on your new position or was Caldwell seizing an opportunity to spotlight his 'workplace inclusion' skills?" asked Clark sarcastically.

"Neither." Elizabeth looked Clark dead in the eyes. "He basically told me not to publish any in depth advance pieces and to simply run an outcome brief after MacDougal is denied. He was cold, he was pushy, and he wasn't taking no for an answer. I have no idea who this guy was or what company he was with. Plus, he knew a lot about you and Richie's visits to the Pentagon. He came here and he knew that we had been to the mine – I don't how but he did."

"We tripped a sensor in the mine the day we went up there and broke in. They knew down in Washington. Richie's source told him." Clark said evenly.

"That explains a lot.." Elizabeth wondered out loud.

"What do you mean?" asked Clark.

"Well, I saw Richie earlier. It seems whoever doesn't want us publishing this story also sent Richie's wife pictures of him and his 'source' sharing more than information. Clark, we are up against some dark forces at play here and they are either connected to or are the actual owners of this paper. I gotta be honest – I don't know what the fuck to do. The one guy who could help us out would be Steve

Miller and you're telling me he didn't help you? Maybe I should still call him…"

"Who came to see you?" asked Clark.

"Some guy named Bromley. He was older, late 70's, maybe early 80's. He was really serious and dressed in a black suit and overcoat. He wasn't exactly the nicest person I've ever met. He told me not to publish your story and called it a directive."

Clark smiled.

"I'm glad you seem amused. You know I'll fall on my sword or jump on the grenade or take a bullet or insert your favorite heroic cliché here– but I honestly don't know how to get around him, Clark. I'm not going to be told what's news and what isn't and because he doesn't want our story to get out it just makes me want to publish it even more – like even if it's the last thing I do. But I don't know what I'm up against here and I don't know how to maneuver around these owners." Elizabeth sounded defeated as she spoke.

"You're asking the wrong questions Liz," said Clark. She tilted her head quizzically as if to say, "how so?"

"Liz, if our story is important enough to attract attention from the owner group to the degree that they threaten you, then the first obvious question is where does their interest intersect with what we've found? Did you ask him why he didn't want you to publish it?" Clark pressed.

"Of course, I asked him. He wasn't going to reveal anything – plus he made the case that puts us in a terrible position which is if our story exposes a litany of mitigating factors and shows some type of cause that may earn MacDougal parole and then we would be responsible for letting a child murderer out of jail. I gotta be honest – no matter how spectacular our details are

that we uncover about CIA experiments or clandestine cold war bunkers, they aren't going to eclipse the outrage if this guy walks out of prison. Then I'll be the first black woman city editor in Newark who got a child murderer paroled in her first week….Jesus."

"So, he got to you," said Clark. His tone was quiet rage. "I really thought you'd last more than the first day Elizabeth. Oh well. I tried. I gave you every opportunity I could and trained you and mentored you in the belief that you wouldn't just roll over at the first sign of trouble. Guess I was too optimistic…" he sighed.

"Oh, fuck you Clark!" shouted Elizabeth. "Put yourself in my place. I'm in a corner here and I'm on your side. You can't blame me for trying to get this story out and still try to not get us fired or worse…!"

"You're right." Clark's tone was calm and smug. "I can't blame you. After all, you've got a lot of pressure on you as editor. Don't worry about it, Liz. Forget about my story, I'll figure out something else to do for my column next week. This is too much pressure for your first week. We wouldn't want to upset the owners. Also, if I get fired, I'm just an old dog who goes home and collects a pension. Don't worry about me."

And just like that Clark rose from his chair and stormed out of Elizabeth's office. She continued to protest as he headed for the door, but he didn't acknowledge her speaking. He wasn't actually angry – but he needed Elizabeth to think he was. She was in an impossible position, and while it was bad enough for her to have to choose between her loyalty to Clark and the pressure from the new owners, neither knew who these mysterious owners actually were and what they were up against.

The darkness of the movie theater cast a ghostly glow over rows of empty seats with ripped upholstery. The floor of the Little Theater looked like it hadn't been mopped in a decade. Two male porn stars dressed as cowboys were about to undress on the massive movie screen behind him as Clark scanned the seats looking for Richie Byrne.

"I'm starting to think you really like coming here for recreation rather than work meetings," Clark said only half joking as Richie sat down next to him. "Do we really have to keep meeting here?"

"Listen man – this is the only truly safe place I know, and we've got some problems so thanks for agreeing to meet me here," said Richie, clearly troubled.

"Well, I gotta update you on a few things…" said Clark, trying not to pay attention to loud sounds emanating from the pornographic movie that was playing before them.

"Yeah, but you aren't going to believe the shit storm I'm in," Richie interrupted. "Clark, after you left Washington the other day, I had a bit of an episode with Kelly."

"Oh, that's how we are going to refer to it? An episode?" remarked Clark while snickering and making air quotes with his hand.

"Look man, don't judge me…" Richie put his head down as he spoke. "Yeah, we had an episode – we got at it again – I thought I could just talk her into getting access to the recruitment records for the MK Ultra prorom, and we went to her house and logged in to CIA and Pentagon mainframes and found some easy to find but pretty important stuff. Then the next thing I know I woke up in her bed and she was making me coffee."

"Hey man – I don't care what you do. I won't judge." Clark was trying to be conciliatory.

"Yeah well, I don't remember any of it Clark," said Richie, sounding exasperated and confused. "But we found a roster from one of the training units that listed Joseph MacDougal and his home address." Richie opened a worn leather briefcase that was on the empty seat next to him and brought out a folder containing several sheets of paper. "I printed these out. You can see they have a column for current addresses next to all the names. The spot next to

MacDougal's name is blank in that column." Richie handed the folder to Clark.

"What do we know about this list of names?" asked Clark as he examined the documents.

"Well this was in a section that Kelly said was the unit that was the group that recruited and trained in Harriman and it covers from 1965 to 1970 – Look here is his name on page three. It is named the 'Cassandra Unit'. Precise tactics aren't listed but this was found in a bigger section of records that covered Autonomous Remotely Triggered Disruption Assets. Sounds like a brainwashed sleeper assassin if you ask me…" pondered Richie.

"Cassandra Unit…holy shit….," muttered Clark. "I interviewed MacDougal again in prison and he told me a lot. He said he was really into drugs in the late 60's and he met a girl he kept referring to as Sandy that he said took him to parties and gatherings at the Lake Sebago camp and they would get high on LSD and do exercises and dances that were a lot like training. He said it seemed really organized. They would do repetitive chants and all kinds of weird things like finding their way back to the mine after they dropped them off in the woods. He also said he witnessed a stabbing."

"You mean the mine we went to that was the COG bunker?" asked Richie as the moaning sounds from the movie playing got even louder.

"Yeah. I don't know if they showed them the inside or not, but he said he had dated a girl named Sandy who used to organize these parties and was kinda the leader, and that once he fled after the stabbing he never saw her again until after the murder when he entered his guilty plea in court.." Clark's voice trailed off.

"OK, well a lot of women with the name Cassandra go by the name Sandy for short," added Richie.

"Yeah, I know. If we assume the association is correct, then this is the roster for the MK Ultra group that recruited MacDougal and the woman who seduced him into it – this Sandy or Cassandra – seems like she was an operative." Clark mused.

"Why would she show up at his arraignment?" asked Richie.

"It's probably closure – and this is probably the date here in the margin – December 12, 1974," Clark pointed to numbers in the margin next to the space where MacDougal's current address would have been written.

"Clark, somebody sent my wife pictures of me and Kelly in bed," said Richie quietly.

"Geez…" sighed Clark. "How did she take it?" he asked compassionately.

"Well…." said Richie and paused… "How do you think she took it….?" The rhetorical question seemed to illuminate the severity of the situation in which they found themselves.

"Well, it gets worse buddy…" said Clark. "Some guy visited Elizabeth and claimed to be one of the new owners of the paper. He knew everything about our story, and he told her not to publish it."

"Yeah, she told me," said Richie. "Why would the new owners not want this published? It's only going to help their bottom line if we break a really big story - what's the logic in that, Clark?"

"The logic my friend, is that whoever this guy is, he has a vested interest in our piece not being published. He is either with the new owners or not, but I have a feeling he wants certain elements of the intelligence community's misdeeds to remain unknown. He is couching it as necessary to keep a child murderer behind bars, but I think it's more than that." explained Clark.

"Yeah, but all this came out in hearings in the 1970's. It's not like what they did back then is unknown – Christ! It's the subject of countless movies and thriller books – documentaries on Netflix – it's about as secret as Area 51 and the Roswell crash. Why do they still care? Why do they care enough to ruin my marriage and strong-arm Elizabeth? And why aren't they coming after you? You're the guy doing all the digging?" Richie's voice was rising as he shouted out his questions in complete exasperation.

"They just haven't found me yet. But they will. I'm not going to burden Elizabeth with this. If they really are the owners, then this should go in another newspaper anyway. I can sell it as a special to the Washington Post and they will buy it. I'll tell them everything. I'm going down there tomorrow," said Clark with a determined tone.

"Yeah, but back up a minute…." Richie put his hands out as if he were directing traffic. "Why does anyone at the CIA still care about this? I'm sure everyone who worked this series of MK Ultra modules is either dead or retired and again – it's all known. We are only providing a local angel.."

"Come on Richie, you are smarter than that…" said Clark. Richie looked at him genuinely perplexed. Clark extended his neck moving his face closer to Richie's so there was no chance the significance of his statement would be lost. "It's because there are more of them."

"More of what?" asked Richie, still baffled.

"Look at that list you've got in your hands…it's pretty long, isn't it?" said Clark, tapping on the paper with the list of names. "These were going on in numerous locations, there were recruitment and training sites all across the U.S. and Canada. That's a pretty lengthy roster of possible assassins – or ticking time bombs – depending on your vantage point. MacDougal killed a seven-year-old. How many names on that list have also killed innocent civilians because of a malfunctioning psychological trigger? They are concerned because there are more Joseph MacDougals out there – some have killed already, and some will kill in the future. That's a lot of messy police investigations and grieving families to keep whatever remains of this Cassandra Unit sweating. They happen to know where

one of their assassins is, and they need to keep him there."

Chapter 10

Melody Westfield removed her earbuds to see what the dog was barking at. Someone had come to the door and likely rang the doorbell – but any sound would have been undecipherable over the pulsing electronic dance music that helped her through the workouts she watched on television. She opened the heavy front door to see an elderly woman slowly walking away from the stoop, down the front pathway and carefully getting into a car. It was a woman she had seen when her father took her to his hometown church several counties away. It was Isabella Della Russo – the mother of the boy whose portrait was on the shrine in the churchyard her dad had shown her. Melody opened the storm door and stood on the front porch.

"Excuse me! Ma'am?" Melody called as the old woman descended clumsily into the driver's seat of her car. Though Melody was calling loudly, Isabella Della Russo refused to acknowledge her solicitations. It was then she noticed the cardboard box that had been left on the steps. "Ma'am is this yours? Is this for us?" called Melody at the still open car where the woman sat.

"Those are for your father," said Isabella Della Russo without turning her head. And then she turned the key in the ignition and drove off. Melody picked up the heavy box and brought it inside to the dining room table. "Case Files" was scrawled on the lid in black magic marker. Inside were folders, loose papers and several yellow legal pads. Just then she heard the metallic wheeze of the hydraulic storm door springs extend and in walked her father with a blank look on his face.

"Dad – that lady from your hometown church whose little son was murdered – the one that Grandpa knew – she showed up and dropped this box off and said it was for you. But she didn't come inside or anything," said Melody. Clark Westfield walked up and looked in the box. On the yellow pads he recognized his father's handwriting. There were several aged and weathered sheets of paper that looked like interoffice memos with Department of Defense letterhead and logos at the top, several others had Central Intelligence Agency logos and William Gottlieb listed as executive director. The contents of the memos seemed to be biological diagnostics of groups of individuals arranged into lengthy tables. The subject line of the memo read "Lysergic Diethylamide Dosage Response Field Studies". In one of the folders was an 8x10 photograph of a large camp cabin identical to the one at the Lake Sebago Civilian Conservation Corps site. "Location 62 Lake Welch" was written in pencil on the back of the photograph. "What is all this stuff dad? And why didn't that lady at least say hello?" asked Melody.

"Mel… when I was a kid, I made a mistake that changed my life and I need to prevent you from making the same mistake right now," said Clark. "Do not look through this box. Don't read the memos. Don't look at grandpa's notes, in fact forget this ever showed up." Clark put the lid back on the box as he was talking.

"Grandpa's notes? These are his papers? That's so cool! Why did that lady have them? Why can't I look at them? If they were grandpa's then maybe there is something cool in them," whined his teenage daughter.

"I guess she didn't burn them after all," muttered Clark as he picked up the box and started up the stairs.

His daughter called to him "Dad come on – what's the big deal?" as Clark ascended to the second floor and into his bedroom. His wife Mary Lynn was on an exercise bicycle in the corner of the room also with headphones on. Clark let the box of legal files land on the bed with a thud. He stood there staring at the closed box and black magic marker in his father's handwriting on the lid.

"Hi hon," said Mary Lynn, still peddling as she put away her earbuds. "Whatcha got there in the box?" She was cheerful and smiling. Clark stayed silent for several seconds.

"This is a box of my father's legal files from the Della Russo murder case," said Clark coldly.

"I thought you kept that box in the attic," said Mary Lynn as her husband continued to stare at the covered box.

"It's a different box mom," chimed Melody who was in the doorway listening unbeknownst to her parents. "That old lady from dad's childhood church – the mother of the dead kid that is always in the news stories just dropped it off on our front porch and drove off. She said it was for dad, but he won't let me read anything in it."

"You want to know what's in this?" Clark said as the volume of his voice rose with anger. "This is evidence of a horrific crime. It's so unspeakable you'll wish you never knew about it. I read the files when I was a kid and I've never been able to forget it. As long as I've lived, this case has haunted me. Can't you just honor my request and please not let your curiosity unleash the same lifelong torment that it caused me…? Can you please just do that for your dad?"

His daughter and wife looked at him with bewildered caution. Mary Lynn spoke first.

"Why did you lend her the files, Clark? Why would a mother want to see that?" she asked gently.

"It's not the same ones. This is a different box. My father prepared these for her and gave them to her. She told me she had them, but she had burned them. Apparently, they survived the flames perfectly," he said sarcastically. As he spoke Melody took several folders and legal pads and laid them out on the bed in an organized line.

"Dad, if you're worried the case is going to freak me out, I read the files in the box upstairs back when I was 12. It's not like I don't know what happened," said Clark's daughter as she continued to empty the box.

"Melody! Why would you do that?" asked Mary Lynn Westfield.

"Well, I wanted to know what was in the box. It's an old case grandpa had from like forever ago. The pictures were gross, but I didn't look at them long," said Melody matter of factly as she lifted two reels of quarter inch tape from the bottom of the box. "Wow hey look – what are these?"

"You read the files upstairs in the attic?!? Goddam it, Mel!!" growled Clark angrily. "Give me those," he snarled as he grabbed the two reels of tape from his daughter. He then began to stack the folders and pads back in the box. A label on the plastic reel tape said in script writing "CW Esq. Statement for the File." Clark put the lid on the box and turned to place it on the floor of the bedroom closet. He turned around to find his wife and daughter looking at him perplexed, saying nothing.

"Mare, I've got to go meet somebody," he said looking out the window.

"OK." She replied. "Who do you have to meet?"

"I don't know," Clark said softly.

"OK...." said his wife slowly and non-confrontational. "Where is the meeting?"

"I don't know," said Clark again. His wife and daughter looked at each other.

"Well, who is it that you are meeting?" asked his daughter.

"I'm not sure," said Clark almost in a trance.

"Well, are you sure they work on a Saturday?" pressed his wife in as gentle a tone she could muster and sensing something was wrong.

"Yeah..." said Clark almost in a whisper. "They are always working....."

Mary Lynn and Melody Westfield looked at each other with concerned bewilderment as Clark Westfield slowly turned and walked into the hallway, down the stairs and out the front door.

Lake Tiorati in the center of Harriman State Park is one of several in the park with a swimming area open to the public. The calendar between Memorial Day and Labor Day is when that lake has a small beach with two lifeguard chairs and a stone cabin pavilion with a snack bar. It looked exactly as it had since the 1930's. The swimming area was roped off with floating buoys at a safe depth. On hot summer days the beach was packed with families. A parking lot across the street adjacent to the circle had fixed iron barbecue grills on poles at hip height. They were so rusted that no food could actually still be cooked on them. But it didn't matter to the hundreds of families – mostly Latino, Hindu and Muslims– who had driven from their nearby urban enclaves and found ways to experience summer ecstasy. Volleyball games were bouncing between groups. Pakistani women clothed in traditional Muslim coverall robes, complete with burkas, served volleys to scantily clad Guatemalan women wearing thongs bikinis and covered in tattoos.

Clark organized his thoughts as he stared at the beach and began walking the route from the lake beach to Bradley Mine. He started writing his story in his head and creating a historical picture of what those times must have looked and how it all unfolded.

The way Clark saw it, if one didn't know better, the present idyllic scene of American multiculturalism in the New York State woods looked as if it could be the updated millennial version of a Norman Rockwell scene. But these exact beaches that now proudly displayed this new harmonious world order had been ground zero for terrifying and traumatic LSD trips, mind control and murder. From 1965 to 1970 groups gathered on the sand and in the main room of the lodge which was now the pavilion. They were shouted at by drill sergeants dressed in suits and in turn shouted back the mantras. They were instructed to catch each other as they fell backward blindfolded. They were dropped off in the woods with a bag over their head and told to find their way back. They were food deprived, sleep deprived, given more LSD, subjected to extreme hot and cold, shouted at more, calmed down with sex from federally paid local prostitutes and then given even more LSD.

And in that five-year patch of Cold War paranoia, young lost souls looking for acceptance and support returned first on weekends and then almost daily. An army nurse practitioner named Cassandra Martin, known to the group as Sandy, had hand-picked each and every individual recruit, making sure the right ones came back . Those chosen first returned for the faux romance and the drugs, then out of habit, and finally with no will of their own. Nurse Cassandra administered the final field practicum for what had become her first graduating class of more than 50 young men and women. On hot sticky July night in 1969, two government officials pulled up in a large sedan and removed a heavy burlap object from the trunk, tied at one end and writhing, twisting and moaning. Inside the burlap blanket was a homeless person that had been picked up by the two intelligence officers. They had given him enormous amounts of whiskey and he was in a state of delirium as they removed the wrapping on the beach sand and the recruits watched.

"Who's the guest Sandy?" said a young Joseph MacDougal.

"This isn't for you sweetheart. Stay up here," said Sandy stroking his face. She walked down onto the beach as several of the others followed her. Joseph MacDougal stayed where she told him to. Sandy then lifted a large medallion from under her shirt and showed it to several of the recruits that had crowded around her. They then drew knives from belt holsters and stabbed the derelict homeless man that stood on the beach. He staggered, drunkenly trying to keep his balance. As his blood streamed through the sand and down into the lake water, the two intelligence officers looked on in approval. The Cassandra Unit had its first graduating class of MK Ultra Remote

Activated Sleeper Assets, and cowering in the corner of the pavilion above the beach was shaking and terrified Joseph MacDougal.

Four years later, in 1973 Joseph MacDougal returned to Lake Tiorati and parked his car. He removed his own burlap sack from the trunk. This one wasn't moving. This one wasn't heavy. This one held the bruised, beaten and abused body of a seven-year-old boy in a scout uniform. And down Arden Road to the faint path that led up a steep bluff, he trudged with little Anthony Della Russo over his shoulder until he saw the entrance to Bradley Mine, exactly as he had been instructed to do. And it was here that Clark Westfield stood in July 2016 after deliberately re-tracing MacDougal's footsteps for what he hoped would be the last time.

Clark searched around the entrance to the Bradley Mine for the spot to scramble onto the rock ceiling. It was there that Richie Byrne and Elizabeth Cranford and Clark had unexpectedly slid down a rocky shaft into the elaborate Continuity of Government bunker that lay under the flooded main entrance. It was here that they had tripped a sensor signaling the high command in Ft. Collins Colorado that controls the nuclear arsenal, which in turn alerted both the Pentagon and the Central Intelligence Agency Joint Office of Contingency Planning. That sensor had brought these clandestine and completely unaccountable shadow government agencies into the life of Clark Westfield. And it was here, after purposely tripping that sensor a second time, that Clark Westfield decided to sit and simply wait for whomever had purposely tried to ruin Richie Byrne's marriage and pressured Elizabeth Cranford not to run their story.

The silence in the entrance room of the mine was deafening. Drops of water falling far into pools of stagnant rainwater could be heard echoing through the two tunnels that branched off. The metal lockers that lined the rocky walls were marked with various symbols – First Aid, Radiation Detection, Food Rations, Water Decontamination. The floor to ceiling gray aluminum locker marked "Bunker Management Manuals and Protocols" loomed menacingly over a dimly lit chamber where Clark's camping lantern created cartoonishly foreboding shadows. Clark sat at the main desk and imagined himself a sort of Armageddon concierge that would check in government officials, bank presidents, foreign dignitaries, a medical staff and various VIP family members in the event of a nuclear launch. Clark stared at the brass plaque on the wall which read the site was commissioned by President Dwight Eisenhower and would "Join the collective efforts to preserve and continue the United States Constitution and its valued principles."

"Clark Westfield….." said a hoarse elderly voice. Clark wheeled around to see an elderly balding man with round glasses and mustache. The lenses of his glasses were so thick his eyes looked enormous, and his facial expressions slightly distorted as a result. He was round – overweight and non-descript with small stubby fingers on meaty hands. "I have to say it sure is an honor to finally meet you in person. We've followed your work all these years and you're one of the best investigative journalists still working. They don't make them like you anymore." The old man smiled as the lantern light glinted off his glasses.

"How did you get in here? And who are you?" asked Clark. Now that the purpose for his visit to the mine was in motion, the adrenaline was starting to surge, and he felt his heartbeat quicken.

"I'm William Bromley. I run a division at Langley that coordinates with an elaborate umbrella of intelligence agencies – but I suspect you already know that." The old man spoke in a friendly but somewhat sinister tone. "There is more than one way into this facility, obviously, so when we saw you driving up here it was just a matter of waiting. You would have made a great asset back in the day Westfield – your instincts for initiating communication are spot on. It's time we had a talk, yyeess…?"

"You're the goon that threatened Elizabeth. Are you also the dirtbag that mailed those photos to Richie's wife?" Clark could feel himself starting to sweat despite the steady cool dampness inside the mine.

"Goon? Really? Come on, I'm on your side Clark. My meeting with Elizabeth was necessary. She is a talented young lady, and you really did a nice job with her," said Bromely with his still smug expression.

"Why did you impersonate the owners of our newspaper? And just who the fuck do you think you are showing up and interloping in people's lives?" shot Clark. The slight pangs of rage accented his voice. Bromley chuckled into a full-blown wheeze.

"Ha! I didn't impersonate anyone! Press International is a company we founded to buy regional newspapers, and I am on its board of directors. We used to only own the big nationals – The New York Times, The Wall Street Journal, The Washington Post – but then when it was clear some of our assets were going to be how shall we say - 'disruptive' - in local communities, I pushed for regional newspaper purchases. With reporters like yourself out there fighting the good fight it turned out to be a wise strategic move."

"What do you mean 'we'? Who is the 'we'? Who the fuck are you people?" asked Clark.

"For somebody so tenacious and brilliant you sure have your share of gaps and blindspots Westfield," Bromley's eyes rolled behind his thick glasses as he spoke. "Intelligence services have always had a hand in media companies – the only difference between everyday news and propaganda is you'll accept information as news because you pay 50 cents for it and it's neatly folded at a corner stand as opposed to being shouted by a demagogue from a podium. Fascists and dictators around the world have always had their grandiose spectacles to feed their megalomania. But every strongman had an expiration date because their power depended on the populous accepting the propaganda as true. Eventually, the crowd notices little details and inconsistencies in that gap between dogma and reality and realizes it's all a show. Then, it all usually collapses in the bloodiest of uprisings. But a free press – As a propaganda tool it has no expiration date and can be molded to suit any situation. People crave it, saying it's an inalienable right in a democratic society, and they are largely correct. What the government and your mentor editor, Mr. Miller, always knew, was that a free press can tell the populace exactly what it needs to hear when it needs to hear it and it will serve as their gospel. All of it builds a seamless narrative that neatly packages American idealism with a bow. Every now and then we let an old dog like you break a story that makes everyone think there are checks and balances. I know you're a purist, but it's been the intelligence community's IV drip of key stories and topic manipulation in the news that has kept America together all these years."

"So, you're telling me the newspaper I worked for is owned by the CIA?" Clark asked incredulously.

"Well not exactly, and certainly not on paper. Let's just say that the intelligence community, to serve and protect American interests, has always exerted influence on the news media. I'm partial to newspapers so I run that group, but we have a robust television division that turned all the network executives into valuable assets over the years, senior programmers in the top 20 markets – and with the advent of cable we can intercept any television station signal at any time if there is a problem." Bromley had an expression of pride as he spoke.

"So, the CIA owns a bunch of newspapers and television stations? How is that even legal?" asked Clark in disbelief.

"It's perfectly legal – in fact it was made legal by an act of Congress in the 40's! You grew up listening to that shrill tone of the Emergency Broadcast System which always seemed to be tested in the afternoon and dismissed as a public service – that was a way for us to commandeer the airwaves and all radio and television broadcast frequencies if we ever needed to. The American people were fine with it and helped us build it! Then, we just took it to another level and didn't tell anyone that we were also 'helping' in the news divisions."

Bromley released a slight chuckle. "We had to stay one step ahead of the Soviet Union at all times, Clark. The threat was constant and acute. It was a global battle between Democracy and Communism. It's simply part of the cost of freedom. And whether guys like you believe it or not, we are all better off."

"Well, I'm glad the era of you suits throwing your weight around under the banner of Cold War righteous indignation is undermined by the internet and social media. You can rig stories all you want but the Cold War is over, and the new digital media is transcendent. Despite all its faults it backs you guys into quite a corner, doesn't it?" challenged Clark. Bromley chuckled again.

"The internet… Oh Clark, you disappoint me. Who do you think invented the internet? It was originally a hardware application that wired bunkers like this with the global network of military bases. You are standing in one of the first sites where the internet functioned, and one computer talked to another. It was thriving for decades in underground facilities just like this one – then I came up with a plan to onboard civilian use once we figured out how to keep track of all content. And social media – do you really think all those prima donna's in Silicon Valley invent those platforms while on their skateboards? No social media app sees the light of day if we can't monitor and seed the platform. You don't think we could take that chance, do you? Plus, social media has proven to be even better than any news story on any media outlet that we could generate – we can communicate directly with whomever we want about anything we want at any time we want. It's a brave new world Westfield, and you and I are in the twilight of our professions."

Clark thought for a minute before speaking.

"So, you're here to tell me that you've been interfering in the routine business of newspapers for years and threaten me not to publish the story that I've discovered of one of your agents going rogue and killing a child?" challenged Clark.

"I haven't made any threats, Clark," said Bromley icily. "But you are correct in that you won't be able to publish your story. Tragic about that Della Russo boy. I remember that night right here in 1973. I met your father that night. He was a good man. Driven, much like yourself."

"You knew my father?" Clark asked, a sudden wash of vulnerability and grief filled his chest.

"Well, we weren't buddies, but we had to keep an eye on him as he put the defense case together. I'll tell you he was a smart man and an excellent attorney, and he probably could have gotten MacDougal acquitted or at the very least gotten a reduced jail sentence. So, we had to have some conversations and be persuasive." Bromley mused.

"You threatened my father?" Clark said defensively.

"Threaten? No." Bromley shook his head. "A guy like your father doesn't respond well to threats, much like yourself. But it also wasn't necessary. He was too smart a man. No, with your father it was simply a matter of discussing the bigger picture and the implications the details of the Della Russo case would have on the public. He understood. Most reasonable men of a certain IQ can understand the greater good that is at stake in certain situations."

"Greater good? What greater good?" shot Clark. "You didn't know my father – he was above reproach! He wouldn't have been intimidated by some government lackey like yourself who wants to play spy versus spy. Pieces of shit like you disgusted him and he worked his whole life to shine a light on the very corruption you're talking about. Greater good.. go fuck yourself." Clark felt a bead of sweat run down his temple. He suddenly fought the urge to simply run.

"You correct on all accounts. Your father wasn't intimidated, nor was he corruptible. In fact, he was a bit of an enigma when we first started auditing his life. Usually within 24 hours we can find various details about a person's life that when confronted gets their attention and cooperation. Most men have a side dish at the office they are fucking like a secretary. Some have boyfriends. Others gamble. Elected officials are easy because they can't get into office without doing things, they don't want the world to see. Anyone that works in intelligence will tell you that under a microscope everyone's life is dirty. And when you have access to their bank records, their mail, their friends, their clergy, their medical records – there really is very little you can't get them to do if you need them to cooperate. But your father – he broke the mold. We couldn't find anything on him. I even accessed his college records and spoke to childhood friends. I thought that there must be something somewhere. But nothing... He was a genuinely good man your father was." Bromley's tone was wistful, and Clark felt a warm surge of pride in his chest.

"So then why did my father abandon the defense that a clergy confession was inadmissible and hide the records of your assassin program?" asked Clark quietly.

"Because Clark," Bromley said softly. "Your father, as pristine and good a man as he was, understood that there was a greater good to be served here. He understood the only thing that is black and white is chicken shit. He understood the bigger picture. As did your mentor Steve Miller who we've worked with for years. And, as I suspect, so will you."

"Greater good!?" gasped Clark. "You fucking people parade around like you are on some moral high ground with your greater good justification – YOU DID MIND CONTROL EXPERIMENTS ON INNOCENT PEOPLE AND IT RESULTED IN THE MURDER OF SEVEN-YEAR-OLD BOY! What greater good could that possibly serve?!" Clark was shouting and it echoed on the rock walls.

"That boy was a casualty of war," Bromley shot back sternly. "Nobody wants anything like that to happen, but it did. The MK Ultra

Program wasn't perfect. That's why it was discontinued. It started out as research, and we didn't give the recruits any assignments or any live triggers. Then the Cassandra Unit, which trained right here in Harriman, activated the triggers for a group of recruits who eventually left and went about their lives. MacDougal was one of them, which meant he was a ticking time bomb if he was ever triggered. He was in the 1-2% that always seemed to malfunction. That's why the program was discontinued."

"1-2%?" gasped Clark. You mean out of the thousands of men and women you plied with your LSD and mind control torture, two in every hundred went on murderous rampages?"

"There were other malfunctions, yes," said Bromley quietly. "Do you really think it's human nature for someone to kill a child? Yet random, unexplained child murders happen every year, don't they? When it's an adult victim it's not as noticeable, and often it just comes and goes as a local news story. But when it's a child, everyone wants answers. And that's exactly why your story can't be published – it doesn't serve the greater good."

"Giving the community answers about why this little boy died doesn't serve the greater good? You guys came clean about this in the Rockefeller hearings in the 1970's. The world already knows what happened and how unethical and brutish you guys were in the name of American idealism. So, what am I missing and what are you still hiding thirty years after your cold war is over?" Clark was trying to reason with Bromley.

"Do you really think Joseph MacDougal was the only one, Westfield?" Bromley asked. "We did a record purge after Watergate and another before the hearings. We did this by the way, with the full approval of the Ford White House administration. But when we purged those records, we lost tabs on several classes of recruits. That meant we were unable to continue to monitor them as they moved to different jobs and around the country. So, by the 80's we realized that we had hundreds of ticking time bombs out there who would malfunction and commit murder and mayhem if their triggers were activated. Usually, we find out after the fact when a seemingly random and inexplicable crime has taken place. At least with MacDougal we know where he is, and he can't hurt anybody else. But he will never leave prison. If the warden unlocked his cell and escorted him out the gate, he wouldn't make it a block. We'd make sure of it, no matter what your story said."

"So then why are you going to such lengths to block my story?" growled Clark.

"Because god dammit!" shouted Bromley. "Because it would cause a general panic and after all - we are the good guy's Westfield! Despite what you hard core ethicists think – despite your hippie idealism, despite your Atticus Finch view of how things OUGHT to be, we are still –and always have been –the good guys. But do I really need to go to any 'lengths,' Clark? But we both know why you won't publish your story though? No, we both know why you're going to go home and pretend this never happened don't we?" hissed Bromley.

"And what reason is that?" asked Clark, genuinely perplexed.

"Because" said Bromley slowly. "Because an eight-year-old Clark Westfield needed an explanation for those terrible photos he saw in the garage that day. And an older Clark Westfield, reassured him that whatever unspeakable thing had happened had been taken care of by his father and that it was all ok now and the bad guy was in jail.

And to publish your story would mean you would have to acknowledge that your father covered up evidence, committed legal malpractice and negligence and wasn't quite the great man that the world knew him to be or that you have idealized him to be. And that would reverse that sense of security and safety he instilled all those years ago, as well as permanently alter your memory of Clark Westfield senior and the relationship you have with those memories you hold so dear. And frankly, we know you don't have the stomach for it." Bromley sat looking directly into Clark's eyes with a piercing stare. Clark felt the bile in his stomach start to rise as his abdominal muscles tightened.

"It was nice to finally meet you Mr. Westfield. You have my commitment that we will be of assistance on future stories down the road. We always enjoyed working with Steve Miller, Ms. Cranford seems very capable. I trust you know the way out." And just like that, Bromley nodded as he finished speaking, turned and walked into the darkness of one of the descending tunnels. Clark stood in the silence, consumed with a sudden tsunami of acute grief for his father and wept like an eight-year-old.

Melody Westfield delicately threaded the fragile plastic ribbon through the flattened plastic wheel. It had taken her three YouTube tutorial videos to operate the old TEAC reel to reel tape recorder she borrowed from her high school audio visual storage. There was a time when every citizen in the United States, and certainly every teenager, knew how to mount quarter inch tape on the spindle, wind it around the levers and snug against the tape heads to the receiving wheel. In fact, in 1974 this maneuver was innate to the average adult, especially an attorney who wanted to get a deposition or a personal statement on the record. And that was exactly whose voice Melody Westfield was hoping to hear. Her grandfather Clark Westfield had recorded something of importance on this tape – something important enough to give to the mother of the murdered boy whose killer he had defended. It was that prospect of grandfather Clark Westfield's wisdom preserved on this brown flaccid ribbon that had caused her to visit her high school on a Saturday, lie to the security guard that she had forgotten several notebooks for an upcoming English literature exam, walk to the AV closet that held several generations and models of household electronics and search until she found a reel to reel quarter inch tape recorder. Placing some loose-leaf notebooks over the antique artifact, she had smiled at the security guard on the way out of school and here it sat, slowly spinning on her dining room table.

The tape hissed a warm sizzling sound as the first few inches wound around the center of the opposite reel. Then, as if a beam of sunlight broke through parting clouds on an overcast day, she heard her grandfather's voice:

"This is Clark Westfield, the attorney who appeared on behalf of Joseph MacDougal, and the contents of these files are evidence that was not introduced in court as part of his defense. I am submitting this evidence to the family of the victim, seven-year-old Joanna Della Russo, as a complete and total explanation as to the circumstances surrounding his death. It was my fiduciary responsibility as Mr. MacDougal's attorney to make this evidence known to the court as possible mitigating factors prior to his sentencing. Should the family of the deceased victim choose to do so, this tape may serve as my on-the-record deposition that I violated my ethical obligation to defend my client by suppressing evidence and I will face whatever repercussions the Bar Association deems appropriate. Because of the elements involved in this case, I leave that decision to the victim's loved ones and family and will honor whatever course of action they choose to take."

The warm hiss of blank tape then returned. Melody pushed the stop button and reversed the direction to rewind the tape. Squiggly unintelligible sounds of her grandfather's chirpy voice playing backwards at a high speed filled the room.

"Don't play it again Mel," said a voice behind her. Melody turned around startled to see her father standing quietly behind her. His eyes were brimming with tears.

"Why not Dad? I want to hear grandpa's voice again," she said as the tape finished rewinding. She pushed play and the warm hiss returned.

"This is Clark Westfield, the attorney who appeared…" her father's finger depressed an adjacent button and the reels clicked to a stop.

Melody looked up at her father standing over her with a curious expression.

"Daa..ad! What's wrong?" his daughter whined.

"Not now Mel, ok?" said Clark softly.

"Jeez! I was trying to help! I thought you'd appreciate it. I went to the school, and they don't even know I took this old TEAC tape recorder. It's grandpa on that tape I thought you'd WANT to hear him! Whatever…!" said a frustrated Melody as she rose from the table and towards the stairs. As she got the entrance she almost collided with her mother, Mary Lynn Westfield.

"Where are you going Mel? Did you show your father that you managed to get a tape recorder?" asked her mother. "Clark – look what Mel was able to do…"

"Forget it Mom, he doesn't care," said their daughter as she stormed out of the room and up the stairs. Mary Lynn Westfield walked up next to her husband and took his hand. She sat at one of the dining room chairs and patted the one next to her in a motion for Clark to sit down. As he sat down, Clark exhaled a deep sigh and put his head in his hands resting his elbows on the table. His wife put her hand on the back of his shoulders.

"What is it, Clark? Did you have the meeting you were hoping to have?" she asked softly.

"Yes," he replied.

"And? Was it helpful? Are they going to give you problems with the story you're working on?" she gently pressed.

"No." said Clark. His hands still covered his face.

"Then what is it? Is it hearing your father's voice on the tape? Is that what's getting you?"

Clark sighed again and turned to face his wife. "Mare, I've got the biggest story I've ever worked on. And I've finally got the answers I've been looking for since that day in the garage when I was eight years old. And with this tape I've got the explanation directly from my father. Even when he was operating outside the law, he was honest and accountable." Tears ran down Clark Westfield's cheeks.

"But that's a good thing then, right? What is the problem?" asked Mary Lynn.

"The problem is if I do the right thing and turn in the story I have, the world will learn what's on this tape – And I will have betrayed my father and all the memories people have of him..including me." Clark's voice trailed off.

"Well, it sounds like he left it up to the conscience of whomever has the tape," pondered Mary Lynn Westfield. "And when Ms. Della Russo gave it back to you, she also gave you that decision to make."

"Yeah, well I wish she hadn't," shot Clark.

"Well why not zoom out for a moment. Clark, hear me out. Your father was a good, honest man. And somehow, after all these years the decision has come down to you as to what serves the greater good and bigger picture. That's always been how you've made all your decisions reporting and that's how your father made his decisions – including the decision to keep whatever files are in this box out of court. Now it's up to you. It's not about whether your father was bad or good or whether the government did terrible things or why some psycho deserves parole or not. Its about which decision will have the best outcome for what happens next. It's against your nature as a reporter to think that way. You are in the business of explaining things, not saving everyone – but that's absolutely how your father thought in making his legal decisions." Mary Lynn leaned her head on her husband's shoulder in a sign of devoted support. "When is the parole hearing?"

"Wednesday," muttered Clark.

"By then you'll know what to do," said his wife. "Either way you know we support you and I don't think there is a wrong course of action here."

"I wish I agreed with you," replied Clark softly.

The warmth of the concrete heated the skin on the backs of Clark's thighs almost to a blister as he sat on the steps of the courthouse administration building in Trenton. The July sun made the expanse of steps a kiln while inside the New Jersey State parole board met to decide whether Joseph MacDougal would be granted freedom after 45 years in prison for the brutal murder of a seven-year-old boy. Earlier that morning, the boy's parents and brother had all filed in, flanked by police officers and attorneys. They had prepared statements in hand with lengthy emotional arguments as to why there should be no parole granted for what appeared to the public to be a violent, senseless, depraved act of a psychopath. A group of several dozen onlookers had shown up, some with signs reading "No murderer walks free" and "Justice for Anthony". Some dressed in scout uniforms to show solidarity. Two television crews weaved in and out of the group of supporters engaging in random interviews with the bystanders, navigating the various shadows and fur-covered boom microphones on poles. The air was electric as the world waited for the parole board's decision. And a dejected and sullen Clark Westfield stared off into the distance as the doors to the court administration building opened and a cackling cluster of people streamed out onto the steps lead by Isabella Della Russo. The small cluster of chaotic humanity stopped midway down the massive steps at the first landing. The supporters and news media crews surrounded Isabella Della Russo and her family members.

"Thank you all for coming, your support means the world to me and my family," she said into a cluster of microphones. "After testifying this morning to the parole board that the man who took our son must remain in prison, we were pleased when the court clerk informed us just several moments ago that the monster who caused us all to be here and caused a lifetime of torment and pain shall remain in prison!" Isabella Della Russo waved a piece of paper in the air over her head as the crowd erupted in cheers. Several broke into a chant of "Justice for Anthony!" Clark sat watching, expressionless.

As the crown dissipated, and the Della Russo family gave the last curbside interviews and shuffled into two waiting black SUVs, Clark opened his laptop computer and called up an email. He addressed the email to Elizabeth.Cranford@starledger.com. And typed "Here you go Liz, he got denied parole. Story attached. – Clark. Then he attached a file from his documents folder titled MacDougal Parole 2016 and hit send. As the screen showed the email had been sent, he continued to sit, feeling a sense of relief that the whole ordeal that had started in his garage as an eight year old was finally over. Living with, accepting and making sense of everything he had discovered in those years and especially this summer was a different matter – and a burden he knew would haunt him perhaps forever. His deep introspective trance was broken by the vibrating ring of his cell phone which displayed Elizabeth's office number.

"Hello? Liz? I just emailed you my story – did you get it? He got denied.." said Clark.

"Yeah, Clark I got it – it's short – it's only five paragraphs and it just says he was denied parole again," said Elizabeth Cranford through the static of New Jersey's crackly cell phone service.

"Yeah well, that's the news. He got denied. Plus, you have a mandate for a 400-word brief right? Just go with that.." he said, sounding dejected.

"Clark, I would have published whatever you sent me. I was ready to take the heat. You want to go with your larger story and the intelligence sources – I'll do it. I've got your back. Please, let's go for it…" said Elizabeth in a pleading manner.

"Nah Liz, we are good," said Clark. "Go with that. I've had a lot of time to think. There are no hard feelings between us. What you've got is the whole story, or at least the story that everyone needs." There was a resignation in his tone only a deflated spirit could create.

"Ok well, we can talk later. But this isn't the whole story. I have another envelope here that arrived earlier – it's a letter from the Administrative Office of the Courts saying that as a perfunctory matter, Joseph MacDougal was today denied parole and we could refer to the statement issued by the parole board in previous hearings. But then there has only been one statement ever issued by the state parole board back in 1992. Gosh this is so confusing….wait..here we go: the New Jersey State Parole Board cordially refers media and interested parties to the 1992 statement which serves in perpetuity as the position of the Board. Hmm… then there is a lengthy multi paragraph letter that has a description of the crime and the effect on her family etc.”

"Well, no one handed out any statements down here so I guess you should take whatever sections you want from that old statement and add them into my story wherever you think it fits. I trust your editing skills. I'm taking the rest of the day off Liz…I need some time," sighed Clark.

"OK – I'll file this and then we can discuss the rest when you get back up here. How do I run quotes from a 24-year-old parole board ruling – do I just say in a 1992 letter?" pondered Elizabeth.

"Well usually the chair speaks for the parole board so you can attribute it to whoever was the chair of the panel at that time. It should be on the letterhead or at the top of the docket – is there a name there?" asked Clark trying to be helpful.

"Oh ok, yeah good idea." said Elizabeth appreciatively. "Here is the name….Cassandra Martin…"

Acknowledgements

I wish to express my gratitude for some people who have been an integral part of birthing The Adventures of Clark Westfield - The Cassandra Unit and other books in the series. Without them, there wouldn't be any adventures. They are:

-My wife and children who were patient both in my writing absences and when I got frustrated with substance and process. They provided encouragement, excellent suggestions and never told me that I sucked or was crazy, despite probably quietly thinking the opposite...

-My early beta readers, Dr. Sandro LaRocca who dove in on the first draft and whose enthusiasm continues to propel Clark's adventures forward. Keith MacPherson, the mindfulness guru form the Great White North who continues to inspire and lead by example.

-The real life abandoned iron mines in Harriman State Park. They inspired me so much that the book practically wrote itself.

-My 8th grade English teacher, who told me I couldn't write and rejected one of my book reports and accused me of plagiarism because it was "too good". You have no idea the damage you inflicted

on generations of impressionable, hopeful adolescents. Perhaps the

bright side is that rage is an excellent motivator to keep one writing.

You should never have seen the inside of a classroom and I pray

every day that your corpse rots in hell.

-My former boss who told me not to write a book because "it doesn't

pay well." Well, I told you not to go into politics….so are we even

now?"

-A special thank you to Jerry Ramos of Mercury Studios in Rahway

who was the first to hear every chapter as we did drafts of the

audiobooks in real time. You were the perfect sounding board,

encouraging, engaged and always hilarious.

-The real life Steve Miller, who has created generations of Clarks and

Elizabeths as the best journalism professor on the planet at Rutgers

University. You not only teach us the news and how to get it, you

teach the most important part – the "why"….

Other mentors, inspirations, friends and general appreciation:

Ray Andersen, Paul Wichansky, Micah Warren, Kieran and Mercedes and Hendrix (and +1), Rick Johnstone, Fred Porter, Ryan Hampton, John Oates, LOURDS LANE, and Brian Peice.

-Sara McDermott-Jain for all her help and guidance and most especially her patience....